Ballers
His Game

Blue Saffire

Perceptive Illusions Publishing, Inc.
Bay Shore, New York

Blue Saffire/Perceptive Illusions Publishing, Inc.
P.O. Box 5253
Bay Shore, New York/11706
www.BlueSaffire.com

Publisher's Note: This is a work of fiction. Names, characters, places, and incidents are a product of the author's imagination. Locales and public names are sometimes used for atmospheric purposes. Any resemblance to actual people, living or dead, or to businesses, companies, events, institutions, or locales is completely coincidental.

Ordering Information:
Quantity sales. Special discounts are available on quantity purchases by corporations, associations, and others. For details, contact the "Special Sales Department" at the address above.

Ballers 1: His Game/ Blue Saffire. – 2nd ed
ISBN: 1-941924-96-4
ISBN-13: 978-1-941924-96-9

Be mindful that the shoes you judge could just become yours.

Ballers

His Game

Blue Saffire

Chapter 1

I am not a hard man to understand. I love my family, and I love the game I have given my life to. Once that was it for me, the field and my family; granted, I was very young at that time. I think maybe if you hear my story you will think about what you hold dear in your life. I never said I was perfect. I made a hell of a lot of mistakes. Mistakes I can never take back or right. None the less my mistakes have made me the man that I am today.

From the time that I was a small boy, football was the only thing that mattered to me. Other than life on the ranch, it was what my family came together around. I was a star athlete in my hometown and everyone got behind me with their support when I became serious about going pro. I didn't think there was anything that would change the way I felt about the game. Now, I know that there are just some things that will change your mind about everything.

For me that was Tamara. That woman turned my world inside out and sculpted the man I am and want to be. To know our love is to know our all access, non-filtered, dirty truth. We just ask that you hear it all and not judge what you haven't lived, but learn from what we give you a picture of.

It's funny how you can find home in the last place you think you ever will. I am a Texas boy born and raised, so when I got drafted to California, I was nervous as hell. To say I was green is an understatement. I had never been that far away from my family for more than a summer camp experience. I was freaked that I wouldn't be able to handle it or make it. I am the youngest of three siblings and the baby of a ton of cousins.

I wasn't afraid of the money so much. My family does well enough in the ranching and oil business, so I was used to having money and managing that part of my life. I guess you could say I got caught up in the test of character and fame that comes with the game.

Everything my mama and daddy taught me was put to the test in week eight of my first pro season. I made fast friends with a few of the fellas on my team, but Troy was my right hand. I guess it was because we were always bunked together. He was in his third year with the team, and he just loved to play and enjoy the life it afforded him. According to Troy, you just keep it plain and simple.

For a while, I followed Troy's advice. I kept it plain and simple and enjoyed my time before the dream faded away, and I had to go back home to Texas. I never thought I would move to second string as a rookie and I sure as hell didn't think I had a chance at starting. I was happy to be in a jersey on a pro team. But in a blink of an eye, one turn of events can change your life forever.

"I need to find some ass tonight," Troy mused beside me at the upscale club.

The club we were in was packed, but none of that mattered tonight. I got to play the fourth quarter, and I threw the game winning touchdown. It doesn't look so good for our starting QB, but that is sort of good news for me. I'm going to get to start next week, at least, according to the doctors maybe even for the rest of the season.

"Good luck with that," I reply. I take a swig of my beer, scan the club, and bob my head to the music.

"Who needs luck, baby? Look around you. Someone is coming home with me tonight," Troy smiles.

"You mean coming to our hotel room," I chuckle. "Maybe you can find one with her own place this time."

"What you need to do is find you a girl to get your country ass to relax," Troy teases. "I'll tell you what. I'll even let you pick them this time. Go ahead pretty boy, I have yet to see you put your Mac down, and I'm interested to see if you are as smooth with the ladies as you are on the field."

"Okay," I laugh taking another pull of my beer. "You're on."

This is the point where I should be listening to my big brother's voice in my ear and my sister's right beside him seconding his sentiments. I had two girlfriends in high school, and both were long term relationships and we remained friends to this day. In college, I messed around with a few girls, but I have remained friends with all of them as well. A one night stand in a city I am leaving in the morning is not me at all.

Instead, I start scanning the room. If college taught me anything, it taught me how to read women. I mean I wasn't completely naïve. I knew a quick lay when I saw one, and that is what Troy is looking for. Me on the other hand, the voices of my siblings are ringing louder and louder. I have every intention of just playing the wingman tonight as usual.

My eyes pass over the sloppy girls with disinterest. Troy may want a sure thing, but he is not into sloppy. I am coming up pretty empty even with the large selection. The girls that don't read sloppy, read trouble, and I am not going to set my boy up for trouble. Just when I am ready to throw in the towel and tell Troy I'm not into it tonight, he is on his own; my eyes lock on the most beautiful woman I have ever seen.

Her head is thrown back, and she is laughing at whatever her friend just whispered to her. From this distance, she looks like a closer look is more than worth it. Her friend isn't bad looking either, but I had to hear if *her* laugh is as beautiful as it looks.

Troy follows my line of sight to see what I am staring at and locks on my target. He laughs and shakes his head. Taking a pull of his beer, he looks at me pointedly.

"No," Troy says and sighs, "Don't get me wrong, I have been watching the one in the blue dress since we got here, but I am looking for a sure thing, that sister right there is not a sure thing. I don't have it in me to work that hard tonight, no matter how fine she is."

"So you take the blonde," I say without thinking.

"Your winter white ass thinks you got enough game to pull that chick right there? In the blue dress," Troy chuckles.

"We'll just have to see," I say and give a smile.

"Oh, I have got to see this. You're picking up my dry cleaning for a month after this one," Troy laughs hard and shakes his head. "You do know those dimples aren't that cute."

I shrug and turn to the bartender to order a bottle of Vintage Champagne and have it sent over to the girls in question. Mark looks at me and draws his lips in an appreciative smile. I just sit back and watch as the champagne is delivered.

~B~

"Tamara, enough already," Stacey argues. "You have had this plan since we were little, and it became a crazy plan after high school. Crazy or not you have pulled it off, so it is time you start living. You are not leaving here tonight without a piece of hot man candy."

I throw my head back and laugh. Leave it to Stacey to be blunt and to the point. She is right. I had planned to be a lawyer since I was a little girl watching my dad. Daddy is amazing; he passed the bar in multiple States and moved on to become a judge. I just knew one day I would be a lawyer, and I would make my dad proud.

The small sacrifice of giving up dating was not as crazy as Stacey calls it. It was the right thing to do to get what I wanted. Distractions are not an option when it comes to your goals. My love life can wait. I'm in no rush to get married or have children. So my decision was never a big deal to me.

However, if you ask my mother, Stacey or my brother, my plan was crazy, and I needed to live a little. Stacey is one of my best friends and she, for the last seven years has made it a point to tell me that I am wasting my life away. I guess having a 4.0 GPA and finishing what I started doesn't count as living.

Stacey on the other hand, at twenty-four, has been engaged twice and married and divorced once already. She is happy being a trust fund baby and spending her divorce settlement. Her inner thighs are as friendly as the girl herself and everyone loves Stacey, so that is pretty darn friendly.

But now that I have accomplished my plan I do feel like I am missing something, so here I am tonight. I let Stacey talk me into coming to this club so that I can, as she put it, 'finally let go and stop being a control freak.' Alright, so that is what I told her I would do. I just have no intention of sleeping with some random guy she picks for me.

I am just going to sit here and watch her get drunk and find her next boy toy and then I am out of here. Knowing Stacey, it won't take long. She got her breasts done last year after years of complaining that I had all the assets in our relationship.

That always makes me laugh. At five-nine Stacey is lean and very fit. She could be an actress or a model with her tanned skin and long blonde hair. She tried once when she was married but Clay, her ex-husband, was too jealous and possessive for it to work.

Stacey's golden green eyes are unique and light up when she is excited about something. She has a cute little nose that comes to a point that could only work on her face. For a white girl, she has a cute little butt, but she is not satisfied with that either. So for the last six weeks, she has been torturing me four days a week. I hit the gym with her to squat her tushy into perfection.

I do it because I love her. Lord knows I don't need any more help with all the junk in my trunk. I have a healthy set of twins as well, and I have managed to keep the rest of my body in great shape thanks to hitting the gym with my older brother to help him rehab in the last two years.

Stacey and I are like ebony and ivory. I am brown skin with chocolate brown eyes and sandy brown hair. I could give Gabrielle Union a run for her money only I am two inches shorter at five-five. So yes, I am one of the very pretty girls as Stacey's mom puts it. I remember when we were younger her mom would try to push me off on her nephew.

I was happy when he got engaged, not that he is not attractive. I just wasn't interested. Besides, Damon used to sniff my hair when we were younger, and it was just weird. I had gotten into the habit of twisting my long waves into buns and wearing hats when he was around. Just thinking about it makes me pat at my loose waves that are floating around my shoulders and down my back tonight.

"Stace, I am only here because it is you… and what happened to Reese by the way?"

"Okay, tell me the last time you saw Reese since she started doing her thing. She's all in love now, building an empire," Stacey says and rolls her eyes.

"I like Nico for her. Admit it, Reese is doing great, and you're just having a moment of hate," I tease and laugh at her pout.

"Okay, so I'm hating just a little," Stacey gives a pout and pinches her fingers together with a tiny gap to demonstrate. "I had a crush on her brother you know. I would have had him too if Kimberly didn't show up all perfect and not me." Stacey can't even keep a straight face with her words.

"You keep believing that, and I'll be helping Christopher with that restraining order," I laugh and throw my arms around my girl for a hug. "I'm glad you're here and thanks, Stacey."

"Oh doll, please. We were potty trained together, started kindergarten together, got our first pointe shoes together, and the list goes on. I'll always be here."

I start to get emotional over our little moment when the waitress appears at our booth with a bucket with a bottle of champagne on ice. Stacey's uncle owns the place and she reserved a VIP booth for us. This place is one of New York's posh spots filled with A-listers, from socialites to models, movie stars, athletes, you name it. I thought the bottle was from her uncle.

"Stacey the two gentlemen over there sent this over," the pretty brunette says with a big smile. I know Stacey's uncle pushes the girls to move the expensive stuff for incentives so she would be getting a pretty something extra tonight.

"Thanks, Danny," Stacey sings giving a sly smile. "There's money in the house tonight." She isn't joking; there is a semester of school tuition sitting on the table before us.

"I think those balloons are starting to pay off," I tease and playfully poke the side of one of her breasts.

"I try, but my assets are still not pulling their weight when you're around, so thank your girls for me," Stacey throws back with a wicked smile.

I laugh at her as she holds out a champagne glass to me. I take the glass and lift it up for a toast. "To the girls," I giggle.

"To my girl who kicked ass in law school and blew the bar exam out of the water. Love you, Tam," Stacey says sincerely and full of the love I know she has for me.

We take a sip then turn to the guys at the bar, and we both tip our glasses in their direction. They hold up their drinks and nod at us. I finish my glass and Stacey refills us both. I guess the guys took our gesture as an invitation because they start to head our way.

They are both tall and well built. They scream pro athletes. Mister Chocolate, as I name him in my mind is handsome and confident. His body language screams player from a mile away. Stacey grabs my thigh and squeals in my ear. "He is hot girl, that is going to be some amazing sex," she gushes.

"Only you Stacey," I shake my head and giggle. I have not held onto my celibacy card for this long to hand it over to some athlete with an inflated ego.

"Hello ladies, can we join you?" Mister Chocolate's silky smooth voice fills the space over the music.

"Under one condition, you have to follow our rules. My friend and I agreed that tonight we want to remain anonymous. That means we don't want to know your names and we are not going to tell you ours. Deal?" This was Stacey's bright idea when she arrived at my place tonight. Being that, I don't plan to hook up with anyone, I agreed to go along.

While Mister Chocolate and Stacey negotiate terms of engagement, I take the time to see what Stacey will possibly be getting into tonight. I know her checklist, and I figure I'll go through it to see if I should just send these two on their merry way now.

Mister Chocolate's friend is the total opposite. Blonde hair, that is kind of long, but not too long. Really blue eyes, that are unlike any I have ever seen. His smile is nice, pretty white and straight, a big plus on Stacey's list. Just as the dimples in each of his cheeks and the one in his chin, that is almost covered by a day and a half's worth of stubble, would be.

His thick neck tells me I am definitely looking at a football player without a doubt. His shoulders are wide, and his arms are large under his blue dress shirt that is rolled up past his elbows, showing off thick tanned forearms. He has an expensive watch on his wrist, drawing the eyes to his tanned skin.

I'm sure Stacey will appreciate the way his dress shirt clings to his muscled body that tapers into a narrow waist. His jeans hug his thick thighs nicely. Stacey will give him points for the three loose top buttons of his shirt as well. He is clearly six-three, maybe six-four.

My eyes take a pass back up and lock with his hungry gaze that is locked on me. I tilt my head studying him then snort. This white boy done lost his mind. I tune back into the conversation and tear my eyes away from the blue eyes that are trying to eat me up.

"Okay, so no names, no personal info. I think we can handle that," Mr. Chocolate says letting his eyes rake over Stacey. *Figures.*

So much for Stacey's great idea to get me some sex. My first prospect is undressing her with his eyes. I frown at Mr. Chocolate when he slides into the booth next to Stacey. I snatch my glass from the table. I have no idea why I am pissed. I had already made up my mind that he is not going to be the one to clean out my cobwebs and lube the pipes.

"Hi, it is nice to meet you," a deep booming voice says beside me.

I turn to see blue eyes staring back at me. Mr. Chocolate's friend has slid in beside me. I look down at his outstretched hand and decide since I am drinking the champagne he and his friend sent I can, at least, be nice. I slip my hand into his large hand, and my palm is swallowed. I don't know what possesses me, but I squeeze harder to not let his large hand dominate mine.

"Nice to meet you," I say dryly.

"Are you just out having a good time or celebrating?"

"I received my passing results from my bar exam today, so I guess you can say celebrating," I reply and look down at our still joined hands pointedly.

"Beautiful and smart," he says with a drawl and a megawatt smile. This man is really hitting on me. I lift a brow, looking him over in amusement.

"How about you," I quiz back. "Looking for an easy lay after a loss or celebrating a win?"

He throws his head back and gives a deep hearty laugh. "Celebrating a win," he smiles.

"Nice, good for you," I say turning my attention back to the dance floor.

Stacey and Mr. Chocolate stand and start for the dance floor. I laugh to myself because Stacey has officially locked down her target for the night. I guess I could just go home now. I look at my phone and groan. It is still early, and I promised myself I would not run out of here too early. I want to say that I, at least, tried to have fun.

"So what made you want to be a lawyer," I hear rumble from beside me.

I turn and narrow my eyes at him. "I have not had enough to drink to sit here and tell you my life story. So let's not and say we did," I say and turn back to people watching.

From the corner of my eye, I watch him signal to the waitress, and she brings him another beer a few minutes later. An hour later he is still sitting beside me having gone through beer after beer. Stacey has not returned yet. I have finished the champagne and have started on the second bottle that arrived. I should feel bad that I am drinking the expensive bottles and ignoring this guy totally, but I am a little too annoyed with Stacey to care.

"So are you ready to talk yet," he says beside me.

I look over at him and his impish smile and laugh. He is seriously waiting for me to drink enough to talk to him. I'm not sure if I should be annoyed, flattered or alarmed. I turn toward him and cross my legs, leaning my elbow on my thigh and placing my cheek in my palm.

"Okay Dimples, what do you want to talk about," I say with a small smile.

He laughs and lifts a brow at me. "Dimples?"

"Yup, that's what I have named you. No names remember," I shrug.

"Okay Counselor," he chuckles. "What made you want to be a lawyer?"

"This again," I sigh. "Okay, my dad was a lawyer and then became a judge. I've wanted to be one too for longer than I can remember. Why football?"

"I never said I play football," he says looking amused.

"You didn't have to, your neck and forearms gave you away," I reply with a laugh.

"You checking me out Counselor," he says with an air of confidence.

It is my turn to throw my head back and laugh. I laugh so hard my belly hurts, and a tear slides out the corner of my eye. He looks at me with mock shock then gives me a half grin.

"You're very pretty when you laugh, but I don't think you checking me out is that funny."

"Aw, Dimples, I'm sorry," I say trying to bite back my laughter. "My brother used to play until he injured his knee, my uncle played for Atlanta for years, and one of my best friends was not only married to a Pro, but her father played for years. So I know a player when I see one."

"Sorry about your brother," Dimples says with real concern.

"He'll be okay. He hasn't been healing the way we all expected so he is going all organic and holistic now and it seems to be working much better."

"That's great. A few of the guys on my team eat organic and all that. I thought about it, but coach isn't big on it, so I haven't done it yet," he muses then takes a pull of his beer.

"It's made a difference for my brother. So... why football?"

"My dad and brother have tossed a ball around with me back on the ranch for as long as I can remember," he says with a reflective smile. "Don't tell anyone but I suck as a ranch hand, so I was never going to be any help to my dad. I guess I always wanted to play ball. I love the game."

I laugh again and give him a genuine smile. His eyes search mine as I laugh. Then his eyes dropped down to the twins that are sort of on display with the way I am sitting. I reach to place my fingertips under his chin and lift his head, bringing his eyes back to mine. "Up here Rookie," I snort.

His brows furrow and he reaches for my fingers wrapping my hand in his. "How do you know I am a rookie?"

I am shocked by the surge of electricity I feel from his touch. I snatch my hand back and wrap my arms around my middle. I shrug and shake my head to clear it.

"It's in the sparkle in your eyes. It hasn't jaded you yet, and it hasn't changed you yet. You still talk about the game with love, not like a job. You're built, but not Pro built and you are still wearing that baby face, which says you just came out of college. You're good enough to play because when you said you won it wasn't just a, my team won, you said it with pride like you had a part in it." I shrug and bite back the smug smile trying to make its way to my lips.

"That is amazing," he laughs. "So how is a woman like you still single?"

"And who says I'm single?" I challenge.

"There is a *lack* of sparkle in your eyes. You are celebrating something great, and if I were your man, there is no way I wouldn't be here celebrating with you. There's no ring on your finger. As beautiful and amazing as you are, any sane man would brand you in any way he could to claim you as his own," he replies with a heated stare.

I feel his words down low. I clench my thighs and squirm a little. Why in the world is it suddenly so warm in here? I fill my glass and gulp it down before looking at him again. He licks his full lips, and I find myself staring at them. I think I have officially had too much to drink, but damn if his lips aren't full and sort of sexy. *Okay, really sexy.*

"Relationships are distractions. Women like me can't afford those kinds of distractions. As soon as you set out to accomplish goals a man just gets in the way. So I made myself a promise to swear men off until I graduated from college, passed the bar exam and landed my dream job."

"So I know you accomplished two of those, how are you doing on the other one?" He asks as his eyes rake my body.

"That would be a checkmate," I say with a smile.

"So you are free to date now," he says with his brow raised.

I laugh and slide over to sit closer to him. He watches my every move with a smile on his face. I look up at him and smile.

"Let's find you a girl so you can go celebrate, Rookie," I chuckle, "How about her?" I tipped my glass toward the bar to a brunette talking to a group of girls.

He follows the line of my glass and points with his chin. "The one in the pink dress?"

"Yup," I let the p pop.

"Nice face, but look at her ankles," he murmurs.

I look down to see she has on shoes that look too tight and her ankles look swollen. My head falls against his shoulder as I laugh hard. I can feel his body shake and hear his rumbling laughter.

"She does have cankles. Oh my gosh. Those poor shoes," I cry. I compose myself and start to scan the room again. "What about her the tall one in black," I point my glass toward the edge of the dance floor to a lithe blonde.

"I plead the fifth," he laughs.

"What? What is wrong with her?" I frown and look up at him.

"I like my women with meat on their bones. Not to mention I'm six five, I think she might be taller than me," he teases. He is clearly exaggerating. She may be six feet tall.

I break into a fit of giggles and shake my head at him. I scan the room again trying to find a better match. He snakes his arm around my waist, splaying his large hand against my belly and points across from us with his beer.

"I think it's my turn," he says against my ear, sending a shiver down my spine.

Maybe I am just sexually frustrated or something. I have to blink a few times when he starts to absentmindedly rub small circles against my flat belly with his thumb. I have all types of butterflies in my tummy. I take a deep breath and follow his gaze.

"The one with the platinum and black shirt," he says.

Once the description is out of his mouth, my head snaps back toward him. His face is mere inches from mine. I pull back a little. "Dimples, the description of that shirt alone cut, blocked and sealed him from ever making the list," I laugh.

He chuckles and looks back at the bar. "Okay," he tips his beer bottle like an arrow once again, "The tall one over there with the other two guys."

I look at the tall light skin guy he is pointing to. He is nice looking, but one close look, and that will be a big no. I look up, start to laugh and shake my head. "Turn on your gaydar, honey. He is batting for the wrong team, but if you think he is cute, I'll go talk to him for you."

He shrugs looks around, then gives me a little squeeze. "What about him?" he nods, and I follow his gesture.

I shake my head and smile. "I actually know him and although he has asked me out a few times before he is not my type," I say with a smile and a wink.

He has pointed out a friend of Stacey's, Paul. He is a nice looking guy, tall, dark hair and green eyes. He works out a lot too. I've just never been interested.

"Meaning he's white?" he asks with drawn eyebrows and tense eyes.

"I guess," I say honestly.

23

"So this poor white boy never stood a chance," he teases and gives me a sad face.

"Oh my gosh, Dimples," I gasp. "You're white?"

He laughs deep, sending the vibration through me. His eyes sparkle when he looks down at me. He bites his lip and shakes his head. "Nope, I think the lighting in here is off," he says and starts to whistle and look around.

I laugh and elbow him in his side. He looks down at me and my lips and gives me that official panty-melting smile. He is still making those darn circles with his thumb. I am ready to lose it. I pull away and slide over a few inches.

"Game over," I murmur.

"Oh no," he says. Sliding to follow me, he places his arm back around me. "We're having so much fun."

I sigh. "If it means I get to find you, someone to go bother, fine." I look out toward the dance floor again. "Look right there, she has a nice rack. Her butt is not bad and she is average height, and since you don't seem opposed to others, she is perfect."

I am pointing out a Hispanic looking girl who really is decent. He looks toward her and sweeps her with his eyes, then holds his hand up in a so-so gesture and shrugs. He looks back to me.

"She's okay, but look at her skirt. It's so short she may moon us if she bends over, which means she is looking for someone to find their way up there, and I would be far from the first and eons from the last."

I burst into laughter and tears. Her skirt is really short, but hearing him say it the way he did with that drawl and his description, I can't help the laughter. I wipe at the tears and place my hand on his shoulder.

"You have to help me out here," I giggle. "What are you looking for?"

He looks down at my mouth and sets his beer down on the table. In the next minute, his large hands are plucking me out of my seat and dropping me into his lap. He rubs his palm up and down my back, searching my face.

"You," he breathes, and I feel it straight to my very core.

I am so stunned that it takes a few seconds to realize he is slowly leaning into me. I blink back my surprise and scramble off his lap. This time, I put more distance between us when I sit back down.

"Listen, it's late, and my family is doing the whole party thing for me tomorrow. I should probably be going," I say and pull out my phone to look at the time.

He reaches into his pocket and retrieves his phone. He swipes his finger across the screen, then looks up at me and frowns. He turns the phone toward me.

"I think your friend left with my buddy," he says almost like he is apologizing for Stacey.

"Oh, um, I'll just take a cab," I reply as I read his text, then look back at my phone to see a similar message from Stacey.

"You had a lot to drink. I have a car waiting for me. I could give you a ride home if you like," he says with concern.

"No, that's fine," I say and stand up. I turn to leave, and the room spins with me. He is right behind me steadying me with his hands on my waist.

I turn to face him and have to take a step back and put my head back. Man, he is really tall, and I have on heels. He smiles down at me and snakes an arm around my waist.

"At least, let me walk you out and make sure you get in a cab," he says with a bit of a plea in his voice.

"Ok," I consent.

I am more wasted than I thought. He stops at the bar to close his tab and pay the bill, asking for a bottle of water for me. I guzzle the water but still need his help walking out of the club. The fresh air helps, but only a little.

"Hey, are you sure I can't give you a ride home? I would feel better if I did, you are pretty drunk," he says with concern.

I look up at him nervously and chew on my bottom lip. He has been really nice all night, and I am probably safer with him than in a cab with a driver I really don't know. I bounce in place as indecision wars in my head.

"Okay," I sigh heavily, and he seems to relax.

He helps me over to his waiting Limousine, and I slide inside. He gets in after me and sits close. I kick off my shoes and lean against his arm.

"You remind me of my brother," I murmur sleepily. "A big old bear, safe and ready to protect, are you soft and cuddly?"

"Not right now, sweetheart," he replies huskily.

I ignore his insinuation and wiggle under his big arm. "Mmm, you'll do just fine," I yawn and snuggle into him.

He brushes my hair out of my face and cups my cheek. "Sweetheart, you have to give the driver your address," he chuckles.

"Oh, right," I say and pop up, "but no personal information."

I crawl over to the window bordering between the driver and us and knock. He rolls the window down, and I lean to whisper my address to him. He chuckles and nods his head.

"You got it," I chirp.

"Yes, ma'am. We'll get you home," he says with a nod of his head.

"Great," I slur and crawl back over to Dimples.

He is smiling at me and laughing. This time, I crawl into his lap and wrap my arms around his neck. His arms tighten around me, and I snuggle in.

"Perfect," I murmur before passing out.

Chapter 2

I feel someone gently shaking me out of my sleep. I open my eyes to find a pair of blue ones staring down at me. I blink a few times, and he smiles.

"You're home, Sweetheart, wake up," he says softly. I try to peel myself off of him, but he tightens his grip. "Here hold onto your purse."

He ducks out of the car, taking me with him in his arms like I am nothing more than a football. He turns and asks the driver to hand him my shoes, letting him hook them onto his fingers. He turns making his way up the path to my front door and sets me on my feet before it. I fish out my keys and open the door, stumbling inside.

"Counselor," he calls from behind me. I look over my shoulder at him and raise my brow in question. "Your shoes Darlin'."

"You can drop them right there," I point. "After you come in and shut the door."

I turn and start for the kitchen again. I hear the door shut behind me then the sound of his heavy footfalls as he follows me. I pull out a glass and pour myself some wine.

"I think my brother left some beer here. Would you like one?"

I look up to find him watching me. "Sure," he replies. "Can I use your restroom?"

"Yeah, first door on the right." I point him in the right direction.

I open the refrigerator and pull out a cold beer and open it. I set it on the counter for when he comes back. I decide to go use the bathroom in my room while he is doing the same in the powder room. When I am finished, I go back to pick up my glass and the bottle and go into the living room. I sit down on one side of the couch, and he sits on the other end nursing his beer.

"Tell me about football without getting into personal information," I say as I pull my feet up and turn toward him.

He gives me a huge grin and starts with his father teaching him the game. I listen to him as his voice pulls me in. The more he talks, the more I sip at the wine and the closer to him I move. Until I am right beside him and my knee brushes his thigh.

"And here I am now, a pro player," he says with a great big smile. "What about you?"

"What about me?"

"For starters, not that I am one, as we established at the club," he says with a smile, "but why the aversion to white men?"

I shrug. "Never really thought about it, I guess I've never really been attracted to one before." I wrinkle my nose thinking about it. "It's not that I haven't thought of any of them as attractive I just never seen myself with a white guy. Don't take it personal. I haven't been with any type of man, white, black, purple, or orange in seven years."

I look up at him through my lashes, and he is giving me that hungry gaze again. This man is really attracted to me, but that is not what is bothering me. I think I am really attracted to him. All of Stacey's comparisons in the differences between different races of men start to roll through my brain. Could I do this, be with a white guy? It's just one night and the thought of his hands on me in the club has me thinking that this may be something I actually want.

The next thing I do surprises us both. I pull my tight blue dress up to free my thighs so I can straddle him and sit on his lap. I brush a lock of hair from his forehead and nuzzle his cheek. His stubble tickles my nose and feels nicer than I thought it would.

"You know you're sort of handsome," I breathe as I tangle my fingers in his hair. "You're sort of really handsome."

I brush my lips across his once, twice, a third time, and he snaps. He palms the back of my neck and nips my bottom lip causing me to moan and open for him. He groans and grasps my thighs, pushing my dress up more.

His kiss is hungry but not sloppy like I was expecting. I don't mind giving him control, I kind of like it. And boy does he take control. He deepens the kiss and cups my butt in his huge hands. I moan, grinding against him.

"Darlin', you had a lot to drink. Are you sure you want to do this?" He pants as he breaks the kiss to look into my eyes.

"If you don't want me just say it, and we can go back to talking," I tease.

He curses and crushes his lips to mine. His tongue sweeps my mouth, and his hands are everywhere. He scoops me up and stands.

"Bedroom Sweetheart, where," he growls.

I point up the hallway, "The door at the end of the hall."

We are in my room with him kicking the door shut in a flash. He toes his shoes off without putting me down or breaking the kiss. Before I can think I am on my back on the bed and he is over me palming and lifting my back with one hand and reaching for my zipper, tugging it down with the other.

I tug the back of his shirt from his pants and pull it over his head not bothering with the buttons. He has his pants undone and shucks them off while I peel my dress down and off. He zeros in on my thong as I go to peel it off next. I peel the damp fabric down, and he groans, biting his lip then looking back up at me.

I smile and reach to push back the covers. He stands pulling off his socks then climbs under the sheets with me. His large frame hovers over me again, and I am so ready. He reaches between my legs testing and teasing me with his fingers.

"I want you so bad," he groans. "Sweetheart, you're so wet."

His mouth is so wet and warm against my neck, my collarbone, and my breasts. I forget where I am, who I am and who I am with. He is consuming me, and I am not sure I know how or want to stop him.

This is not going to work for me. It has been too long, and I want him now. I push his hand away and grab for him, cradling his hips with my thighs then pulling him in.

I cry out with the shock of his size and the discomfort from being so tight. I wasn't expecting so much. I guess some stereotypes aren't as true as they seem. He groans in pleasure anchoring his hands in my hair and then goes to work.

I gasp in surprise as he rolls his hips and bucks into me with long deep strokes. I look up into his eyes, and they are so intense and focused on me. His mouth is slightly open, and his breath is warm against my face as his short bursts of air burst from his parted lips.

Those lips, they are so sexy. I lean up to lick his lower lip and then bite it. He growls and reaches one hand to grasp my waist and quickens his pace. He is so long and thick I can feel him bumping up against my cervix with each thrust.

"Baby, you feel so good," he groans, burying his face in my neck.

The moment I feel his tongue glide up my neck trapping my sweat and hitting my spot I gasp and gush around him.

"Yes," he grunts as my sex squeezes him. He plows right through my orgasm.

I have never, and I mean never, had a man serve my body like this. If I knew sex could be like this, I would have never given it up. I lock my fingers in his silky hair and hold on for dear life. I am drowning in this man as he licks and sucks at my neck.

"Oh God," I gasp. "Baby please."

He lifts his head to look into my eyes before capturing my lips in the hottest kiss ever. I have to grab his rock hard back to keep from floating away. He feels amazing inside me.

He breaks the kiss and shifts, lifting my legs over his broad shoulders. I cry out as his penetration deepens. Oh my God, this man is trying to get into my throat. I find purchase in his thick locks of hair only to tighten my hold when his mouth clasps around my breast.

I'm so wet if he were a smaller man he would probably slip right out. His girth is so thick that he is anchored inside me as if he has just found his home. His powerful strokes rock my body. I swear I'm going to need a new mattress and headboard if he keeps pounding into me like this.

"Oh my God, oh yes," he groans, rolling his hips. I lift to meet his strokes using muscles I haven't used in so long they are screaming back at me. I marvel at the mix of pleasure and pain.

"That feels so good," I moan.

"You're so wet and tight. Your pussy is so good," he growls.

"Your dick is amazing," I moan out of sheer sexual insanity, but it is the truth.

"I need you to come for me again," he says with that sexy drawl.

All he had to do was ask. My drunken body answers on demand. His curse bellows through the air as he pumps his hot release into me, lulling me into a deep bliss. Yeah, he worked that.

~B~

I wake to the buzzing sound of my phone. I turn my aching head and crack open my eyes to see it glowing in the pocket of my jeans that are on the floor. I run a hand through my hair and inhale. All I can smell is her. I reach for my phone and answer.

"Dude, where are you?" Troy's concerned voice comes through the phone. "We need to be at the airport in an hour."

"Shit," I run a hand through my hair again and look to make sure I haven't woken the beautiful woman beside me. "Can you do me a big favor, just throw all my crap in my bag and take it with you? I'll meet you at the airport."

"Sure, man. I'll see you there, just make sure you get moving," Troy chuckles.

I hang up and turn to look at her again. She is sound asleep. I want to stay. I haven't had enough of her. Last night

37

was amazing. I take in her bare chocolate shoulder and want to wake her to show her how much I still want her.

Then it hits me. We hadn't used one condom, not a one. I must have come inside her, at least, a dozen times and I never even thought about a condom. How could I be so stupid? She was so drunk, I was too, but I still had sense enough to know better. I swipe my palms down my face and groan at my stupidity.

I don't even know her name. With that thought it all hits me. She didn't even want to give me a chance last night because I'm white. Why would I think I should stick around for her to wake up and throw me out? She didn't want to give me her name so she sure as hell isn't going to give me her number so I can call her.

My decision is made, I get up and grab my clothes and go into the bathroom. I slap some water on my face and gargle with some mouthwash before getting dressed. Once dressed, I walk back out into her bedroom, going to peek at her one last time.

She is knocked out with her long sandy brown hair splayed across her pillow and a few strands across her face. Her full plush lips are slightly swollen from my kisses and one of the most erotic, sensual and downright nasty blowjobs I have ever had. We can put that black girls don't like giving head myth to bed. I think black guys made that up to keep us white guys away from finding out what true bliss feels like. I have never come so hard.

I couldn't help myself, I bend and kiss her lips one last time before I leave. She stirs a little causing the sheet to shift and her breasts to be exposed. I think again about staying, but thoughts of her rejection and Troy's sage advice play in my head.

"Keep it simple," I mutter to myself.

I have a plane to catch, and I need to focus on starting for possibly the rest of the season. I pad quickly out of her room and down the hall, slipping out of the door. The limo is still sitting there. I tap the top of the car and climb inside. After instructing the driver to head to the airport, he pulls off. I feel like the world's biggest jerk.

I left without saying a word or leaving my number. I drop my head in my hands and let out a bitter laugh. She didn't want a white guy, but last night when I was inside of her, I made sure she knew it was me no matter my color. She was right there with me every step of the way.

I swear something pulled inside me as she looked into my eyes and cried out in pleasure. I wanted to own her. Each time she called me baby it slammed into me. I wanted it to mean something to her, not just a name she had to use because she didn't know mine. I wanted to be hers.

When she was on top of me with her palms on my chest, and she looked into my eyes, with her beautiful brown eyes, calling me baby I forced myself to hear her saying Brad. I wanted her to know my name is Bradley. Images of last night assault me, her in my arms pleading for more.

Me losing it with the need to brand her as mine, like I knew any sane man would. The way she rode me, rocking her hips and grinding on me like I was the best ride she ever had. I loved the way she sucked her bottom lip between her teeth and looked at me like I meant something to her.

It was in that moment that I got lost, believing for just that point in time that I was hers, and she was mine. I felt a connection with her I never felt with anyone else. It had caused me to swell inside her with a force I have never known. I reached up to tug her head back and watched her ride us both into bliss. Her breasts bounced in my face as I rolled my hips up into her hot sex. She was so wet; she

dripped between my legs and down my balls. It was amazing,
....and I just walked away.

Shaking my head, I try to think straight. I smile to myself
as I can't rid my mind of more thoughts of last night. The
huge bite mark she is going to wake up with on the back of
her neck is probably going to piss her off, as well as the ones
on her belly, the one on her inner thigh, and the two on her
ass. Who knows where else I got carried away.

I know it was childish, but she and anyone else that sees
them will know that, for at least one night, I owned that
beautiful body. That beautiful brown skin turned purple
under my bites. God, the woman, even has sexy feet.

I make my plane, exhausted, horny as hell from thoughts
of last night and disgusted that I walked out without leaving
my number. We didn't use condoms. I really should have left
my number. I want to see her again; that should have been
reason enough. I blew it; I know I did.

I went from wanting her when I first saw her to the need
to have her, and now I'll never have her again. I've never
discriminated when it comes to women. A beautiful woman is
a beautiful woman. However, she didn't want me, and I have
to accept that and let this go.

I don't feel like talking on the plane, but that doesn't stop Troy. He is grinning like a fool, which tells me he had a good night. He nudges me and pulls my ear bud from my ear.

"So you'll be getting on that dry cleaning this week," he chuckles. "Did I see the girl you ended up with last night? You were sitting with the ice queen the last time I looked in on you."

"You saw who I went home with," I grumble. "I'm pretty sure you went home with her best friend."

"Wait, get the fuck… seriously. You went home with Stacey's friend? That bad black chick?" He looks at me incredulously.

"Wipe the shock off your face," I gripe. "Wait, the blonde told you her name?"

"Yeah, I wasn't sticking my dick in her unless she did. Anyway, I don't believe you. Prove it," he accuses.

I sigh and shake my head. A part of me doesn't care if he believes me. I don't need to prove it. Then there is the part of me that knows she didn't want me because I am white, and that part of me wants to show that, for a few hours, my color didn't matter to her. She had been picky in the first place, but she let me inside her body, not any other man.

I pull my phone from my pocket and open up the picture I took when she fell asleep in my arms. You could see the side of her beautiful face while the other side was pressed against my chest. You could slightly see the top of her bare shoulder through her long hair above the sheet, but that was it.

I hadn't taken the picture to prove anything. My brother had texted me; I retrieved the phone to make sure it wasn't an emergency. I had been admiring her lying across my chest for longer than I cared to admit before I decided to take the picture. I wanted something to remember her by.

"I'll be damn, you pretty motherfu –," I cut him off when I grab my phone back. "I didn't think you had a chance. I didn't think anyone did to be honest."

"Me either, trust me," I huff.

"Well, was it not good, cause you look like you just got told your dog was run over," Troy asks and really looks concerned.

I laugh humorlessly. "I didn't get her name or her number. It was the best sex of my life, and I just walked out. I should have woken her or left my number or something."

"Oh nah, one night and you pussy whipped. You did the right thing. We'll take you out this weekend and find you a nice little snowflake to help you feel better," he laughs.

I frown at him and put my ear bud back in. If I would have listened to what my family taught me, I would have the number to the girl that somehow stole my heart at first sight. Listening to Troy and 'keep it simple' has me heading to California empty-handed and feeling stupid. Suddenly I realize how much I miss home. Last night was the closest feeling I have had to being home in a long time.

Chapter 3

It's been seven whole weeks since I woke up in my bed all alone. No note, no nothing, nothing but the scent of his cologne on the pillow next to me and a sore body as my proof he was ever there. I thought we had some kind of connection that night. It wasn't just sex. At least, it wasn't for me. He turned out to be amazing, the way he paid attention to me and my body.

The fun we had together during those few hours in the middle of the night were not just some random hook up. I never laughed and connected with a guy like I had with him. We talked and fell into a comfortable zone.

Well, I guess I was wrong because he walked out without a word after. I was stupid enough to spread my legs and let him in. That night keeps haunting me at every turn no matter what I do. The embarrassment from it goes on and on.

I arrived at my parent's house that following evening for my party and was totally humiliated. I'd worn a spaghetti strap yellow sundress; I had bought weeks before just for the party. It was a hot day and night, making the dress perfect. That is until my mom walked up behind me in the yard. I had been sitting thinking about Dimples leaving without a word, and I had started to perspire in the heat. I absentmindedly scooped my hair up and clipped it up with a clip from my purse.

My mom pinched my ribs and giggled in my ear. "I see you finally decided to have a little fun," she chortled.

I wrinkled my nose and looked over my shoulder at her. "What do you mean," I asked confused.

She threw her head back and laughed. "Tam you may want to put your hair back down. You have passion marks all over you," she laughed harder as the color drained from my face. "Oh, baby you didn't know. There is a huge one on the back of your neck and one here," she poked my back. "And one is peeking out here." She poked the side of my dress by my ribs.

I closed my eyes and swallowed hard. "Oh mom, I am so sorry," I reached to tear my hair back down to camouflage. My mom fluffed my hair and arranged it to help hide the marks. I had seen the one on my inner thigh this afternoon and the two on my belly and I thought it was funny until I got annoyed again that he left and didn't say anything.

"Sorry for what," my mom sighed. "You are a beautiful woman, and obviously, you found someone who is passionate about that beauty. You worry about what everyone else thinks and wants too much, Tamara. Your father and I are proud of you. Now, will we be meeting this young man today?"

"No, mommy," I said sadly, realizing for the first time how much knowing that I wouldn't see him again hurt.

"Tam, look at me. You have always made decisions that were right for you. We all may not agree with them when you make them, but in the end, you always make them work. It amazes me every time, and I wonder what I did to get such a special daughter." My mom brushed a lock of hair behind my ear.

"Thanks, mom," I said and gave her a fierce hug.

When I got home that night, I stripped down and found the map of Dimples' journey around my body. Who does that? I wish I could believe in my mother's words now. Since that night, all my decisions have seemed to bite me in the behind, like not wearing protection. I had to be wasted. I would never do something like that. I have known since I was sixteen that I have an allergic reaction to birth control. My doctor tried to regulate my cycle with it and, needless to say, it didn't go so well.

I should have taken a morning after pill or something, but I didn't even remember how stupid I had been until three days later. When Stacey cornered Reese and me to spill all the details of her night with Dimples' friend, it hit me what I had done. She was busy going on and on about him being hung like a horse and that's when the memories hit me. I couldn't remember one condom being used, but I could remember orgasm after orgasm where I went over the edge and I felt him follow.

So I am not surprised that there is a test in my bathroom that is screaming at me that I am pregnant. This was not a part of my plan. I am supposed to be starting my new job and paving my way to partner in the firm. A baby was never part of that plan, but silly me, not only did I sleep with the guy. I let him leave me with a baby.

I have sat here crying for two hours. I'm pissed he gets to walk away, and I have to stay and face the consequences. I've thought about googling what teams played that Thursday night and which ones won then checking their rosters but every time I go to do it I stop. He left. He doesn't want to be found. I'm sure he definitely doesn't want to be found so that I can tell him he has a kid on the way. He probably has a trophy girlfriend at home, and I would just be ruining their life, just like I ruined mine.

I cried all I can, and now it is time to face reality and call in the cavalry. I text Stacey, Reese and my girl Alee 911 and ask them to come over. I look a mess, and they take notice right away. One thing we don't do is look a mess. Alee has been doing my hair since forever. To see me tossed about is a shock to her.

"Okay, so are you going to tell us what is going on," Reese asks raising her brow at me. She is tapping away at her phone no doubt reassuring Nico that she is fine. The man is crazy about her and never lets her out of his sight.

Thinking of the tall Italian man that has taken over my friend's heart makes me think of my own situation. Nico is gorgeous and I never once questioned my friend's choice. So why do I have such a problem dating white men myself? If

Dimples had stuck around would I have really been open to a relationship with him? Well, it doesn't matter now.

"What I'm going to tell you, you can't share with anyone. Ellerie is going to lose it," I say as tears well up in my eyes.

Alee sits silent but frowns at the mention of my brother. I don't have time to sort out that drama today. As if reading my mind, she schools her expression and nods.

"Okay, sweetie, you know I won't say anything you don't want me to," Reese says with sincerity and concern.

"Whatever it is, please spit it out, you have me breaking out in hives," Stacey complains.

"I'm pregnant," I blurt out as the tears run over.

"Wait, what," Reese gasps, "The ball player from the club?"

I bite my lip and nod, trying to hold back the sobs. Reese looks like the wheels are turning in her head. Reese is a problem solver; it is a part of her nature and the reason she is so good at business.

"Okay, so we just tell him. Troy text me the other day asking me to meet up before playoffs start, I can ask him to pass a message along," Stacey offers.

"No," I shake my head.

"Maybe Nico knows him and can talk to him or tell us more about him. I know they play different sports, but Nico and his brothers know tons of people. If they don't know him, I know his brother can find him. This Troy guy, what team is he on? He can, at least, give us a name," Reese suggests.

"No, no, no, I don't want to know. He walked out. He didn't say anything, and he didn't leave a way to contact him. This is not his problem. I'll handle it on my own," I sniffle.

"So you plan to keep it right," Alee asks. "I mean I never thought you would be the first, but I just can't see you doing anything other than keeping it."

"It's my baby," is all I can say.

"Well you know I am here for you whenever you need," Reese says soothingly.

"My sentiments exactly," Alee chimes in.

"I wish I could say the same," Stacey says with a distant look on her face. Reese, Alee and I all look at her like she is crazy. "Oh Doll, not like that, I mean I'm here whenever you need me, but I just won't be here, here, as in New York. My dad is pissed about me burning through my divorce settlement and my trust and he has some clauses he is threatening to use to cut me off if I don't move to Texas where he can keep an eye on me." Stacey sighs then shrugs.

The wheels start spinning in my head and my plan snaps into place. My baby may not be able to know who their father is, but maybe I could do the next best thing. He had let out that he was born and raised in Texas. I could tell in the way he talked about it that he missed home. It must be a great place to grow up.

I could give my baby that, to know a part of where their father is from. I need a change. I need a fresh start.

"I'll come with you," I tell Stacey.

"What? To Texas, are you serious? But what about your job, you wanted to be a lawyer?" Stacey says half excited, half concerned.

"I can take the bar exam there and find a job. My dad can probably help. There are just as many athletes in Texas as there are in New York. I can travel if needed. I want to go. He was from Texas I think it would be kind of cool to have the baby there," I shrug.

"You do know Texas is huge. It's not like you are going to run into him at the grocery store or something," Stacey says and presses her lips.

"I'm not going there to run into him at the grocery store," I huff.

"I think I get it," Reese says with a smile. "I also think you can't hide forever. These things have a way of coming out."

"Reese, you of all people should understand why I'm doing this. What if he has someone that loves him? I don't want to drop a baby on her doorstep, and I don't want to come in between them."

"He had no problem coming in between your legs," Alee snorts.

"Ugh, why do I bother," I laugh for the first time in days and put my head in my hands.

"You're really coming to Texas," Stacey squeals.

I nod and give her a smile.

"You heifers are leaving me," Reese frowns.

"Like you have time for us anyway, Tam wouldn't be in this mess if you were there that night to save her from me," Stacey chides.

"And why do we associate with you again," Reese teases.

"Girl you stole the words from my mouth," Alee laughs.

"I have no idea," Stacey says and looks at her nails like she is bored, and then looks at Reese and Alee, giving them a big smile. "I'll miss you guys."

"I'll be back at least once a month to get my hair done," I say pointedly to Alee then look at Reese. "We can hang out then unless you get Nico to move to Texas," I wiggle my brows at Reese.

"Not happening, have you met the man? He is fierce about his family. So unless one of his siblings moves to Texas, it's not happening," Reese chimes. She is right. From what I know, Nico's family has been through a lot, and they have become inseparable, much like Nico and Reese. "Speaking of which he has been asking if you are ready to take on some new clients. So when you get yourself together know he has your back with a few clients, and I will be spreading the word that my girl is handling business."

And just like that, I became a Texan.

Chapter 4

Five years, it has been five years of torture. I think about that night often, and there isn't a day that goes by that I don't think about her. I have tried to move on and see other people, but I always find a reason that they are wrong, mainly because they are not her.

They're not short enough, not curvy enough, or not smart enough. They don't make me laugh; they don't understand the game or anything about it and not one of them has been as good in bed as she was. Those full lips, her big brown eyes, her cute button nose, it was all perfection. I haven't found one woman to match those standards.

The first year I couldn't even get it up without imagining it was her. I tried everything, dating all colors, shapes, and sizes.

Nothing would do. The second year I took a break from women altogether and focused on the game.

I had a great career in Cali. I was the starting quarterback, and my team was the team to beat. We actually walked away with the ring last year. I had some great endorsements, and I did some modeling here and there. Still, none of that mattered. For five years I felt like something was missing. I lost a piece of my soul, and it was out there somewhere roaming around without me.

I wasn't going back home nearly as much as my family, or I would have liked because I felt ashamed of what I had done. Any one of my family members would have read it on me and called me on it. All I had was a picture on my phone to comfort and taunt me. I made sure it was uploaded to my phone every time I upgraded. I had it printed out and blown up. I did things with that picture that made me look like a stalker or a whipped pussy, as Troy called me until he got traded off my team the year after I met my little lawyer.

But it was all because I knew I fell in love with her at first sight. She owned me the moment I laid eyes on her. I did go looking for her once. It was a few months after that night. I rented a car once I got to New York and drove to her place.

I'd gotten the address from the car service that drove us to her place that night.

When I got there, there was a for sale sign up, and they were having an open house. She lived in a really nice neighborhood. I entered the house to find the real estate agent and an older man who looked annoyed. One look at the man and I knew he was related to my little lawyer. It was in the bow of his lips the way he wrinkled his nose and the almond shape of his eyes.

He had to be her father or uncle or something. He already looked pissed off so I didn't think walking up to him to say. "Excuse me, I think I slept with your daughter or maybe your niece a few months back. And well, I don't know her name, but I think I love her, and I want to find her," was going to work. So I did the next best thing.

I took the tour of the open house with the realtor and feigned interest looking around for clues of why she was moving or at least where to. I came up with nothing and felt sick to my stomach when I left. I didn't think I knew enough about her to hire professional help, and I didn't know how to explain it without being embarrassed.

So for five years I have just managed to exist. I tried a long term relationship thinking that would help. Tiffany was a nice girl she just wasn't *her*. I hated the way she laughed, and she pushed too much. Wanting to meet my family, wanting to move into my place, wanting to be on my arm when I had to show up at events; I guess for a girlfriend all that wasn't a lot to ask. Six months passed and I wasn't in love with her. I was barely tolerating her.

I hated how she would show up at my place and leave things around trying to mark her territory. I'd find strands of her bleached blonde hair in my sink after I cleaned the sink out. Her underclothes would be in random places, and my housekeeper would find them. I just had to end things, and that was true for so many things. I wanted out. So as soon as an offer came my way to go home and play in Texas, I jumped on it.

I shocked everyone. My GM didn't see it coming, my coach didn't have a clue, and even my agent was stunned that I wanted to take the offer and leave. I just needed to go home, find myself, and be with my family. I needed to be surrounded by people that really care about me.

It feels good to be in my parents' home surrounded by laughter and home cooking. I see my dad relaxing and enjoying just kicking back and not worrying about the ranch or drilling sites for once. That is my cousin's responsibility now. My parents bought a great place with plenty of space for them and the grandkids.

I love my nieces and nephews. Watching my brother and sister with their families makes me wonder if I'm missing something. I watched the guys on the team that would rush home from games to be with their kids, especially on holidays. At twenty-eight, I want more, and I see how happy it makes my parents to have a full house.

"I am so happy you are home honey," my mother coos as she enters the kitchen. I have been sitting at the kitchen island on a stool looking at houses on my mobile device.

"I'm glad I'm here too," I say with a genuine smile. It does feel good to be home.

"I hope whatever has been bothering you can be solved with family and love," my mother says knowingly.

Leave it to my mother to get right to the point. This is why I have stayed away for so long. My parents have had that look on their face from the first day I got here. They know something is really eating at me.

"I hope so Mama," I sigh.

"Your brother wanted to come by, but something came up with Donna and the kids. Ann said she and the kids would stop by a little later," she informs me with a warm smile as if she had been reading my earlier thoughts. "So you think you'll be able to find a house close by? You know you are welcome to stay here as long as you like or go to the ranch and stay there if you like."

My mom is great at multitasking. She is preparing dinner for the family, getting games and movies out for the grandkids and tending to me and my issues. I miss being pampered and fussed over as the baby in the family.

"I plan to look at a couple of places tomorrow. Hopefully, there is something promising with those. Things are going to get busy soon. If I can find something early this week, it would be best," I sigh and draw my hands down my face.

I have been looking at houses for a few days, but the problem is that I'm not sure what I want. I know I'll know it when I see it. I wouldn't mind being closer to my parents. I also think I need something that I am going to make permanent.

"Well, just remember not to rush into anything hon'," she says gently sharing her wisdom. "You're home now; you can take time and fix everything that needs fixing."

"Yes, ma'am."

"Now I got all that organic stuff you've been eating, and I changed out the pantry so you can be comfortable while you're here. I want you to always feel welcome without worrying about what you're going to eat," she stirs something in a pot then covers it and goes to retrieve a bottle of water. Placing it in front of me, she takes away the empty bottle.

"I really appreciate it all Mama."

"You're my baby, it's not a problem at all," she stops and looks me square in the eyes. "Whoever she is, if she is the one you'll find your way back to her. If she's not the one you will learn to let go."

I am speechless. I blink back the tears and rest my head in my palms. It's good to be home, this is what I needed.

Chapter 5

"Come on Tam just pick a dress already and put it on," my brother calls from his perch on my bed while I stand in my closet trying to figure out what to wear.

"Ellerie, don't rush me. I don't want to go to this in the first place."

According to my brother, I need to start dating. So his bright idea for the day is to take me to some family and team function at the stadium. He was blessed to have signed a contract three years ago. When the offer came, and he saw the opportunity to play, move to Texas, and be able to look after my daughter and me. So he jumped on it.

He is in great shape these days, and he has always had the talent. His team just hasn't had the right pieces to bring home the championship. I worry about him sometimes because the clock is ticking and the chips seem to be getting further and further away. I know he has done everything he can to stay in Texas because of us, but I want him to go where he will be happy.

"That's exactly why you are going. Just think all that potential money under one roof and the opportunity to talk to some adult men that are not your clients," Ellerie croons.

"That sounds like a contradiction," I grumble and step out of the closet. "If they are potential clients then don't they fall into the same category as all the other men I talk to?"

"Don't they fall into the same category as all the other men I talk to?" Ellerie mocks. "The point here is that you have spent the last five years doing nothing but taking care of my niece and working like mad to become partner. I am proud of you for finally taking a vacation, but when are you going to find some type of social life. I'm not saying dude needs to move up in here or anything. I just want to see you happy."

"Who says I'm not happy? And what do you think of this dress? Is it too much," I ask and spin around as I push my diamond studs into my ears.

I have on a simple black dress that is off the shoulders, fitted in the bodice, flaring out at the waist into a pleated skirt. The insides of the pleats are white with a white petticoat underneath made of organza. The dress falls to just above my knees. It has a classic look to it.

"You're my sister anything you wear is perfect. And you are not happy," Ellerie narrows his eyes at me.

"Uncle Eli," my little monster coos as she runs in the room at the perfect moment and jumps onto the bed lunging at my brother. "Do you like my dress?"

"You look like a princess," Ellerie beams down at her and strokes her silky curls.

Brielle's hair is just one of the many things she got from her father. It's not golden blonde like his but more of a dirty blonde. It's full and thick like mine, but it is silky like I remember her father's being when I ran my fingers through it. She has a natural curl that causes her long locks to fall in Shirley Temple-like curls.

Brielle has her father's blue eyes, a little version of his nose, his cleft chin and two dimples. Only way you know I had anything to do with her is in the bow shape of her full little lips and the almond shape of her big blue eyes. You can also see me in her thick eyelashes and full brows, despite them being a dirty blonde.

Then there is her complexion, she is not brown like me or tanned like her father. She has a mocha complexion of her own that makes her big blue eyes sparkle something fierce. But make no doubts if you see a picture of her father you would know she's his little girl.

Brielle bounces off the bed to do a little twirl for her uncle in her little cotton yellow dress with a satin sash at the waist. My family spoils her every chance they get; Stacey included. My parents spend more time traveling the world since my dad retired, not that I blame them. They worked hard raising Ellerie and me, and they deserve to enjoy their lives. But when they are home, they are usually in town fawning over Brielle.

I named her Brielle after her father and my brother. It was never my plan to find out who he was or his real name. It just sort of happened. For weeks, I tried to avoid pro football events and potential clients. I figured if I stuck to entertainment law and other sports for a while I could avoid putting a name to the face.

Unfortunately, I had a complete meltdown during Christmas with my family, when my brother insisted I hang with him, my uncle, and my dad, watching the game. There his face was flashing on the screen for a California team, Bradley Monroe, on the offensive line up as the starting quarterback.

I sobbed so hard everyone thought I was losing it because of the pregnancy hormones. I had just told them that I was expecting, and there were mixed feelings about it. My mom was excited and welcomed the idea. Both my dad and Ellerie wanted to know who the father was.

I wanted to give my baby one more thing that belonged to her father, so Stacey and I started playing with different girls' names. I didn't like Brandy, so I went with a little of Bradley and a little of Ellerie, hence Brielle.

"Uncle Eli, Mommy, said you are making new friends, and you're taking us to meet them," she chirps.

"That's right beautiful. Some new friends and some old ones," Ellerie smiles down at her.

"Do you think they will like my dress too?"

"You and your mommy will be the prettiest ones there."

Brielle giggles and bounces on the balls of her feet. I love this little girl so much. I walk into the closet and slip on a pair of red satin, platform, peep-toe shoes. Stepping over to the mirror, I sweep on some red lip gloss and smile. My skin is glowing from two weeks on a Disney cruise with Brielle. I am glad I decided to just do black eyeliner with mascara and a touch of black shadow in the corners. I look refreshed.

I grab my red bag, big enough for Bri's reader, my reader and some snacks for my picky eater in case she doesn't like what is served at this thing. She drives me crazy with her picky eating. She's tall for her age and when she eats, she can pack it in, but it has to be something she likes.

I don't know where she gets that from. Sometimes I just want to pull my hair out, but then I remember that I know exactly where she gets it from. I just wouldn't know him well enough to know for sure that I am right.

"I feel so unprepared," I complain. "You guys just got a new player and it's a big deal isn't it. I should have at least gone online and caught up."

I had promised myself I would not look at anything sports or entertainment related while on vacation. I only knew about the new player because Ellerie was excited about getting some help finally. This event would be sort of a meet and greet for all the new guys and families to get to know each other.

"You'll be fine. You are technically still on vacation, and you made me promise not to let you next to the sports section or a broadcast," Ellerie laughs. "Relax Tam, you know I have your back. Once I tell them you are my sister and the best attorney ever you will be making partner in no time."

Chapter 6

I was not expecting this. The paparazzi has come out in full force, which makes my stomach turn. I should have at least looked to see who this new player is. For the paparazzi to be out like this, it has to be a heavy hitter, and this could be huge for me. I am one big client away from sealing partner. I usually don't work with football players, other than my brother. However, to make partner, I am open to all new accounts.

It's not like me to be unprepared. I feel so off, but each time Brielle starts chirping away to her uncle about how much fun she had on the cruise I know it was worth it. You would never know Bri will just be turning four. It's like talking to a miniature adult.

She even negotiates with her grandfather and sad to say she bests him most the time and my dad is still sharp as a tack. Daddy says she reminds him of me when I was her age. If that is the case, I am in for it.

We step from the car and start inside. I rush forward, holding Brielle's hand tight, letting Ellerie have his moment. I can hear them behind me calling out questions about who I am. Who is the little girl with me?

Ellerie good-naturedly tells them I am his sister and attorney, Tamara Hathaway and the little girl is his niece, Brielle. They call our names trying to get us to come back and pose with Ellerie, but I am not going to subject Brielle to that. We make our way inside and out to the field where a large tent is set up with tables and chairs under it.

Players are milling about with their families, and some of the wives are standing in groups talking. I look around for a familiar face but don't see too many as of yet. That's when a slender woman approached me. She is tall with too big hair and too tanned skin. Other than that she is dressed to the nines in her pale blue spring dress and heels.

"Monica Davenport, I am on the committee to welcome the wives and the girlfriends today," she says, looking down her nose at me and holding her hand out limply. She raises her eyebrow pointedly as if to ask which category I fit into.

"I'm Tamara Hathaway, Ellerie Hathaway's sister, and this little lady is my daughter Brielle," I say and take her hand to shake it.

"Oh yes, thought you looked a little familiar. Hello there, Brielle," she says with a pasted on smile.

"Hello," Brielle beams with her chipper self.

Monica looks down at Brielle, and something crosses her face for a moment. Her brows draw together and her lips part. She looks from Brielle to me then composes her expression like it never happened.

"There will be some activities for the children later. You may want to mingle with some of the girls," Monica offers.

I feel a hand on my shoulder blades and relax. Ellerie to the rescue, he always shows up at the right times. "Hello Monica, I see you have met my lovely sister and niece," Ellerie says smoothly.

"Yes, it is a pleasure."

"Thank you for welcoming them, we'll let you get to the others," Ellerie takes my elbow and leads me away.

"Why is everyone staring at me like that," I whisper to Ellerie.

"Because you are the best looking woman in the room, and you look too much like my twin to be my girl, so they're worried about their husbands and boyfriends," Ellerie teases and chuckles.

"You are so bad," I giggle.

I love my brother. He knows how to make me relax and have a good time. He has a loveable personality. It's hard to be around him and not be in a good mood.

We make our rounds with Ellerie introducing me, as his sister and attorney to players I haven't already met. Soon business cards and phone numbers are being exchanged. A lot of the guys are really nice.

I end up in a small group people watching. Eric and Teddy, two of Ellerie's teammates and good friends, flank my sides giving me comical commentary on the owners and their wives. They are making me laugh so hard my stomach hurts. I use my fingers to dab at the tears when Teddy does his impersonation of one of the women who looks like she would rather be anywhere but here.

I am actually having a good time and haven't noticed that time is flying by until my stomach starts to grumble. Teddy raises a brow at me and smirks. "I hope you are not one of those women that don't like to eat. You would be ruining my fantasy," Teddy teases.

"Ha, and here I thought you were a loving and devoted husband," I retort.

"You can be but so devoted when your wife insists on entertaining the pool boy, gardener, chef and any other warm body that enters the residence," Teddy shrugs. "I thought that if I plan to hire you, I should hit on you before the wife does."

I gasp then laugh. "You're joking."

"Am I?" Teddy says with an uninterested shrug. "Let me know if you want to handle the hours for the divorce."

"Wow, I'm sorry Teddy. You are such a nice guy," I say sympathetically.

"Tam, have you met my wife yet? I knew better and still went there. I got what I deserved. But in the beginning, it was worth it," he says and wiggles his brows.

I burst into laughter. "You are so bad," I chuckle out.

Teddy raises his glass and does a mock bow. My stomach grumbles again, we all laugh. Just then Ellerie and Brielle walk over with big smiles on their faces. They are just coming back from watching a little magic show that was put on for the children.

Ellerie wraps his arm around me and kisses my forehead. "Maybe I picked the wrong two to keep an eye on my little sister," Ellerie says with feigned suspicion as he looks between Teddy and Eric.

"Don't look at me," Eric snorts. "Your sister has that look in her eye that you get on the field. I am in favor of my life, thank you."

"Oh, Eric, and I thought we were going to run off into the sunset together," I tease and give Eric a coy smile, batting my lashes.

"See, she's dangerous I tell you," Eric says with a hand to his chest and a mock look of horror.

"Stop torturing my friend, Tam. Eric doesn't know how to act around pretty women," Ellerie chuckles.

"Mommy, your tummy is talking," Brielle giggles as my stomach speaks again. All the guys laugh.

"Go eat something," Ellerie leans over to whisper. "I have Ellie; we'll be right here."

"Are you sure? You took her to the show. I can take her with me. She doesn't want any of it but maybe I can trick her into eating a little something," I whisper back.

"I've got her. You will just be starting a war trying to get her to eat here, now go," Ellerie says and gives me a nudge.

"You're the best big brother in the world," I chime and kiss him on the cheek.

"Whoa, are we starting a line for those," Teddy says and bends down pointing at his cheek.

I swat at his arm and bend to run my hand over Brielle's hair and kiss her on the cheek before straightening and walking toward the food spread. I have perfect timing. I noticed when we were joking around that the crowd had shifted toward the other side of the tent.

I guess the new player creating all the buzz must have arrived. I found out it's a new QB, but I never got a name. Each time I thought I would I got interrupted or the subject was changed without me getting to ask. I am just really excited for Ellerie. This could be big for him as a wide receiver. The old quarterback was one of the biggest issues for him the last two years. Their on field and off field relationship was tumultuous, and the team wasn't willing to part with either of them until recently.

I load a plate up with finger foods while the coast is clear, and I don't have to fight a food crowd. I spot a table where I can rest my feet and eat in peace and set off to the corner to have a moment to myself. I don't get many with Brielle and work constantly tugging at me.

~B~

With the big upset of my free agent signing with a Texas team, I was expecting the big press turnout. Today would be the official announcement confirming the rumors of my new contract. While I'm excited to be home and on a Texas team, it's bittersweet that they choose to make the press conference today at a family meet and greet function.

My brother and sister couldn't make it because of their family's schedules. My mom and dad just aren't up to such an

77

event, five years ago maybe but not today. Tiffany has been calling again and for a moment I was tempted to invite her out, but then she would think things have changed. She would definitely want to meet my family if she was in town, not going to happen.

So here I am alone playing nice with my smile painted on, pouring on the charm. To the outside world I am doing great, but inside this is the last place I want to be. After sitting down with the press, I am ushered into the main tent where the food is set up with all the families and important people to brush shoulders with.

I have shaken more hands than I can count and had more conversations than I can remember, but still can't remember what any of them were about. I laugh in the right places and respond in like manner, but I am somewhere else. I've spent the last twenty minutes trapped listening to one of the sponsor's daughters complaining about her trip to Paris last week or last month, whatever.

The general manager's wife dumped me off with this group before whispering to play nice. Guess news of my breakup has hit. Suddenly inviting Tiff out doesn't seem like it would have been a bad idea. At least, that would have kept the vultures at bay. I wouldn't have to play nice with this group of women I have absolutely no interest in.

As that thought runs through my head, I hear a chorus of laughter. There is the distinct tinkling of laughter that throws me back in time. In that moment, I was back in bed with *her* it was after the second time we had made love.

I figured out she was ticklish. So I was tickling her beautiful little feet. I loved how the moonlight spilled into her room making her brown skin glow.

Her flat stomach taunted me as she laughed and scrambled away from me. She was looking up at me with her eyes sparkling. The joy I saw there turned from laughter and amusement to lust and desire. Her laughter made my heart swell so much I had to have her again and I did.

I reached for her ankles and dragged her back down the bed toward me. I kissed my way up her belly pausing to suck at her smooth stomach. She squirmed beneath me and sighed her pleasure. My eyes flicked up to lock with hers, watching her face as I branded her with my mark.

I pulled her thighs apart and climbed up her body not breaking eye contact. My whole body quaked as I slipped into her warm heat slowly. Her shapely legs wrapped around my back and I felt her little feet lock over my butt cheeks. She dug her heels in urging me to go deeper as she rocked her hips up into me.

I shuttered at the feel of her walls grabbing and squeezing me. She was so tight and wet it was driving me insane. I looked in her eyes, and she looked back at me, watching me with her lips parted. She was so beautiful my breath shuttered to a stop. I cupped her face and kissed her longingly. I never wanted this to end. I was already inside her, but I needed more.

"Baby, yes," she moaned against my lips.

"You feel amazing," I groaned.

I shake the memory from my mind and whip my head around to search for the laughter that brought it back. I hear the joyous noise again and zone in on a small group a little ways across the tent. There are two men and a woman. She has large curls pinned around her head like a crown, but that's not what gets my attention.

It is her shoulders. I would know those shoulders anywhere. I have spent five years obsessing about those silky smooth chocolate brown shoulders. They are now glowing in the off the shoulder black dress that is hugging the top of her body and showing off her legs in a pair of sexy red heels.

I shake the thought off; there is no way. I am imagining things. The woman's back is to me, and I want it to be her so badly that I am making things up. It couldn't be her. Bethany, the sponsor's daughter, pulls me back into the conversation and out of my reverie.

"Bradley have you been to Paris," she asks touching my arm.

"Actually, I have been a few times when I was younger. My mother loves to travel, and she would take us on trips when my father needed us kids out of his hair," I reply.

My response sends her into another long-winded tale about her family's travels. My attention is drawn by that laugh once again, and I just stare. At that moment, another man and a little girl walk up beside her. The girl takes the woman's hand, and the man wraps his arm around her, kissing her forehead.

I feel physical pain at the sight. I have no idea if it is really her, but the thought of her being with another man hurts so much more than the thought of never seeing her again. I watch as they interact with the group and then the one with his arm around her whispers something to her.

"Bradley, I think you should join us on the yacht sometime. Daddy loves to get to know the players. We can trade numbers," Bethany coos drawing my attention with her hand against my chest.

I reluctantly pull my eyes away from the group across the room and turn back toward the group I am standing with. The guys are looking amused, and the women look expectantly at me. I'm not sure what she'd just said, but I go with what I think is the safe response.

"Sure," I reply with a smile.

"Great, give me your phone," Bethany beams holding out her hand to me.

I raise my brow at her in question and stare down at her hand. One of the players, Rodney, stifles a laugh and shakes his head at me. I know I just missed something important, and my answer may have been wrong.

I look at her red finger-nailed hand again then up at her expectant green eyes. I guess you could say Bethany is an attractive girl. Not too thin, nice curves, not that I believe them all to be real. She has big blonde hair that I am sure is assisted like her breasts. She has a false tan, and too much makeup on, which takes away from the appeal instead of adding to it for me.

"Hand me your phone silly, so I can program my number and send me yours. I'll give you a call sometime to invite you to Daddy's yacht," she says like I am a child needing her overenthusiastic help.

I mentally kick myself as I pull the phone from my pocket and hand it over to her. I don't want to be rude now and tell her no. With a smile on her face, she programs her number in, then grabs my arm and pulls me close holding my phone out to snap a picture.

"Smile," she sings before snapping a couple of pictures. "Great, we look good together in this one," she coos. "I'll just text it to my phone, and then I'll have your number and a pic to remember you by."

"If you all would excuse me, I see some friends I want to say hi to," I grab my phone and make an exit while I still can.

I cross the room to the group I had been watching but sometime during the phone incident the woman disappeared from the group. The man she had been hugging is still here as is the little girl. As I get closer, I realize I know the guys, Teddy, Eric, and Ellerie.

I know Eric, the best of the group. I played with him for half a season before he was traded here. I know Teddy through a mutual friend back in LA, and Ellerie is the reason the team wants me here. I have been in meetings with him over the last few weeks as the team made their pitch.

Ellerie is a great wide receiver and from what I can tell a really cool guy. We hit it off right away; there is just something familiar and welcoming about him. I haven't been able to put my finger on it yet, but I feel like I know him from somewhere. It dawns on me as I stop to join their group that Ellerie was the one with his arm around the woman. He is now standing with the little girl in his arms as she is talking to the guys in her little voice.

"It was great. He pulled a rabbit out of his hat and a quarter from behind my ear," she gushes.

"Speaking of quarters the man has arrived," Eric announces grabbing my hand for a shake and pulling me in for a hug. "Good to see you."

"Good to be seen," I nod back and take Teddy's hand as he mimics Eric's gesture.

"You want to tell us something, Monroe?" Teddy says looking at the little girl in Ellerie's arms and then at me. She is looking up at Ellerie still talking away with her back to me. "Oh man, I think I just stepped into a fun house."

"Do you ever shut up," Eric snorts and shakes his head. He then leans back to get a view of the little girl, tilting his head and lifting a brow, "But you have a point."

"You two need help," Ellerie chuckles. "Ellie, this is one of my new friends Brad," Ellerie says to the little girl who turns her attention to me.

"Hi Brad," she says with a beaming smile.

The kid is gorgeous. Her big blue eyes sparkle as her cheeks dimple. Her large curls bounce around her cute face, and her mocha complexion has a glow like she recently spent a lot of time outdoors. She takes my breath away. Eric and Teddy are right; she does look like she could be my kid.

I look from her to Ellerie, and it is clear he is her father. She has his bow-shaped mouth, his high cheekbones and a hint of his smile. There are other things that link them here and there. I pull it together and reach out my hand to her.

"So nice to meet you, Ellie," I say with my first genuine smile in I don't know how long.

"It's actually Brielle," she says with a shy smile, "but you can call me Ellie if you like."

"Brielle, that's a beautiful name for a beautiful girl."

Just like that, she reaches out to me like I'm a magnet and leaps into my arms. I catch her as she sails into my arms, shocked by her sudden move. Ellerie shakes his head and laughs.

"Monroe, we're going to be needing those child support checks," Teddy gives a booming laugh.

"I don't think Ellerie's wife would appreciate that," I retort.

"Actually, Ellie's my niece," Ellerie laughs.

I narrow my eyes at him then look down at the little girl in my arms smiling at me. A million things run through my mind. There is no way. This little girl has to be at least five or six. I think back to six, seven years ago. I was dating Rebecca my last year in college off and on. Rebecca was paler than me with thin lips and a long nose.

I look at Ellerie examining his face. His eyes are a hazel color and are sort of almond shaped. I pinch my eyes closed, trying to see the one face I know that could be similar to his... *no, it couldn't be*. I look at the little girl again. She's too old I continue to tell myself.

"I wouldn't mind becoming a part of your family," Teddy chuckles.

Ellerie grimaces, "I wouldn't mind another visit with your wife," he bites out.

"That's fine as long as your sister is bent over in front of me as I watch," Teddy says casually and shrugs.

"Fellas," Eric places a hand on both their shoulders and nods toward Brielle. "We have a little lady in our presence."

Brielle is more focused on watching me. There is an innocent curiosity in her eyes. Ellerie shoots Teddy a warning glare and folds his arms across his chest.

"Ellie, I think I saw some cake and ice cream being served over there. Would you like to join me for some?" I ask.

She gives me the cutest little pout that reminds me of the one my oldest niece perfected. "Thank you, but no thank you, Mr. Brad. Mommy said I can't have any because I won't eat the food," she says sadly.

Ellerie runs a hand over her head, and she turns to look at him. "How about we run an audible, you and Brad go that way," Ellerie tips his head to the side. "I'll intercept mommy, so you have time to eat your ice cream and cake. Just don't spill it on your dress."

"Oh, Uncle Eli, really, can I?"

"Sure baby, but remember it's our secret," Ellerie says and winks at her. "Brad, if Ellie gives you a hard time just scream for help."

"Oh, I'll be good. I promise," Brielle says with wide eyes.

I don't know what possessed me to offer to take her for cake and ice cream. The kid just drew me in. I tighten my hold on her and start for the refreshment table where I saw them serving cake. I think about what she said about her mama not wanting her to have it because she wouldn't eat and detour toward the food. She is fidgeting with my tie peeking up at me every so often.

"So Sugar, why won't you eat any food," I ask gently.

"Mommy says I'm a picky eater," she says wrinkling her nose. I know I have seen that look before. She shrugs her little shoulders. "I don't know if I'll like it. You shouldn't waste food."

"You know what? I'm a picky eater too. I ate a few things here, though. How about before we get your ice cream you eat a little? I'll get you a plate of what I had, that sound good?"

"Okay," she says, nodding enthusiastically.

"Are you allergic to anything?" I ask not wanting to give someone else's kid something that would harm them.

She wrinkles her nose again and looks me in the eyes as she thinks. "No," she replies. "But when I go see Nana and Pop Pop I have to wash my hands after I eat my peanut butter crackers before I touch Pop Pop or his things."

Feeling certain, she understands what allergic means and that she isn't allergic to anything. I place her on her feet and fill a plate with some turnovers, wraps, and pigs in a blanket. There is a variety of things to choose from, but I go as kid friendly as I can. Plate in hand, I take Brielle to a table, help her into a chair and have a seat.

"Okay, Sugar, let's see if your taste is as good as mine," I say and wink at her.

She grabs for the turnovers and starts to munch away. It is easier than I thought. She sits humming and watching me. I watch her just as intently. Her lashes are blonde but so long and thick. Her hair is not a golden blonde like mine, but it is a dirty blonde color with sandy brown highlights.

"Do you go to school Ellie," I ask.

She nods in between bites then covers her mouth with her small hand. It is such a ladylike gesture. "But Mommy let me skip two weeks to take me on a cruise," her eyes sparkle when she says, mommy.

"Oh really, I bet you had a lot of fun."

"Oh yes, I did. It was just Mommy and me, and I got to go swimming, see movies, play, take princess pictures. At night, me and Mommy sat in our room and read our books on our readers while having quiet girlfriend time to unwind," she says animatedly.

Yeah, this kid could not be mine. She is definitely too old to be mine. I sit quietly to watch her devour the rest of the food. She cleans the plate, which leaves me chuckling. I have no idea where she packed it all. We clean up and then we go to get our cake and ice cream before returning to our seats.

"Mr. Brad, thank you. This is so good," she chimes as she shoves ice cream and cake in her mouth.

"You're welcome, and you're right, it is good," I chuckle.

"I think we should tell Mommy to get a cake like this for my party. Will you come with me to tell her," she says excitedly.

"Sure Sugar, what kind of party," I ask.

Her whole face lights up. That's when I really look at her. Her eyes aren't just blue. They are the exact same blue as mine. Not that I haven't seen people with blue eyes before outside my family, but my family has a distinctive blue. They're not just blue they are midnight around the outside and bleed into a turquoise then light blue around the irises. When they light up from our excitement they almost glow, just like hers are doing right now.

"My birthday party, it's going to be a princess party," she sings.

"How old are you Ellie," I have to know.

"I'm three, but I'll be four in a few months for my princess party," she gushes then her face lights up more like she just had the best idea ever. "Oh Mr. Brad, will you come to my party? You're my new friend you have to come."

I am stunned into silence. Could she be confused? My nieces and nephews were nothing like her at three or four, and she is so tall. I feel like I am talking to a small adult, she has to be older. Her being older would release this pit in my stomach.

Her face falls when I don't answer her question, and she places her spoon on her plate and pushes the little bite left away. I snap out of it at the sight of her crestfallen face. She wipes her little hands on a napkin and slides out of her chair.

"Brielle," I croak then clear my throat. She turns her little face toward me and looks at me with sad big blue eyes. "I would love to come to your party, but we have to ask your mommy and Uncle Ellerie first, okay?"

Her full megawatt smile comes back, and she nods her head with excitement causing her curls to bounce around her face. She launches herself at me and wraps her little arms around my neck. Something tugs in my heart and I am happy I could bring that smile back to her face.

Chapter 7

"What did you do with my daughter?" I narrow my eyes and look around the crowded tent.

Ellerie just strolls over to me like he owns the world. He throws an arm over my shoulder and squeezes. I fold my arms across my chest and give him a pointed look.

"Will you relax," Ellerie says and rolls his eyes. "I love you and that kid more than life itself. I've known where you and she have been every moment we've been here. You do remember I've got the tall gene. I can see over the crowd unlike you."

"Oh shut up," I giggle. "I've had to hear about you and your tall gene and your hazel eye gene since we were little. I don't know why I even like you. You spend more time teasing me than anything."

"You sister dear, love me. And you love me because I tell the best jokes, babysit whenever you need, and I kick anyone's ass that tries to step out of line," Ellerie says, straightening his jacket and his tie.

"Whatever," I laugh. "Where's Bri?"

"I sent her on a mission to have fun, something I'm hoping to get you to do," Ellerie says nonchalantly.

"I think I'm doing good. I was having fun talking to Teddy and Eric," I retort.

"Teddy is in a bitter marriage, and I almost had to kick his ass for even having thoughts of trying to bring you into that mess. Eric is …Yeah, those two are not the type that I want my baby sister with. Besides, they're my best friends we talk a lot of trash to each other but they know how I feel about you and Ellie, and they wouldn't go there."

"What, I'm not good enough for your friends," I put my hand on my hip and scowl. "I was thinking about going out with Teddy and his wife."

Ellerie's mouth pops open, and he glares at me until I can no longer keep a straight face. I throw my head back and laugh. Ellerie tugs at a loose piece of hair at my temple.

"Dad called me last night. They're on their way back home from Greece," Ellerie swiftly changes the subject.

"Good, so they'll be in the States for Bri's birthday. I was thinking about going to New York after her party."

"You won't have to," Ellerie sighs. "They are thinking about coming here for a while."

"Oh Eli, what's a while," I whine.

"Not sure, a few months maybe," he shrugs.

Not that I don't love my parents and want them around. It's just my father has never been happy that I refuse to tell them who Brielle's father is. He always gives me this knowing look, like he figured it out or something. But like a good lawyer, he is willing to wait for the truth to reveal itself with time and observation. That's the problem. My dad is too observant, and he does things to trip me up when I'm not on my game.

Well, he can bring it on because that is one cat that will never be coming out of the bag. Brielle will keep them plenty busy with her insistent talking and demands. Bri can be the little diva when she wants.

"I guess it is about that time again," I sigh. "I just thought I would have this partner thing under wraps, and it would be enough to pacify Daddy for a little bit."

"Dad is just like the rest of us, wanting to see you happy," Ellerie says with a warm smile.

"When are you going to be happy Eli?"

"You'd have to understand my world to know why I do the things I do, Tam," Ellerie says somberly. "You know a lot about the sports world, but there are some things I hope you never find out. I'll get a ring or two, and then I'll go after what I want. Hopefully, it will still be there waiting for me."

"What happened, Eli? When did we forget to be happy?" I muse aloud.

Chapter 8

"Can we go ask my Mommy now," Ellie pulls away and beams up at me.

"Sure, let's see if we can find her and your uncle," I say and hold out my hand for hers.

I stand and scan the room for Ellerie. I lock eyes on Ellerie talking to the woman in the black off the shoulder dress again. Once again her back is turned to me. I have to see her face.

I start in their direction, dragging Ellie along with me. I peek down, and she is smiling up at me with hope in her eyes. She holds her tiny fingers up on her free hand and crosses them. I laugh and give her fingers I'm holding a gentle squeeze.

When Ellerie and the woman in black come into Brielle's view, she rips her hand from mine and shoots off toward them a few feet away. I feel the loss of her hand in my heart. After that everything else seems to happen in slow motion.

I watch as Brielle's curls bounce on her head as she sprints forward. For the first time, I notice her little feet in her sandals as they slap the ground pushing her forward.

"Mommy, Mommy," she chimes aloud. And then the woman turns and sends my world spinning with her. Her face is glowing as she looks down at Brielle with a face splitting smile. Brielle's arms shoot out and wrap around her legs as she collides with them.

In that moment, I feel my knees go weak. I reach out for the back of the chair nearest me to support my weight. I can't believe it is *her*. I am staring at the one woman I thought I would never see again. That's when everything starts to fall into place, slamming into me like a Mack truck.

I'm a father. I have a daughter, a beautiful little girl with my eyes, my dimples, and my chin. I have a daughter with *her*, and I left. I left without a word, without a trace and I have a daughter. I never knew about her because I made the biggest mistake of my life. *Her,* she is the woman that stole my heart in one night looking more beautiful than I remember.

I suck in a sharp breath as I watch them. Brielle says something to her, and her smile collapses. Her eyes draw up in the direction Brielle came from, and her eyes lock with mine. She just stares for a moment, and then she blinks a few times and stumbles backward reaching out to grab Ellerie's hand.

Ellerie's face goes from concerned to confused, his head pops up to follow her gaze, and his face turns to rage. Her hand shoots to his chest, and she turns to say something to him as she shakes her head. And that's when I snap out of it, I can't wait any longer.

~B~

"Mommy, mommy," I hear Brielle singing from behind me cutting Ellerie's and my conversation short. I turn in time to lock eyes with my little girl. Her little legs carry her right to me as she barrels into my legs, wrapping her arms around them.

"Mommy, I ate the food. You would be so proud of me; I ate it all. And I had ice cream and cake, and it was so good. Uncle Eli's new friend and my new best friend, Brad, said he's a picky eater too, so he only gave me what was good to eat," Brielle squeals so fast my head spins.

When her words sink in my smile crumbles, and I look up in the direction Brielle just came from. There he is staring back at me holding on to the back of a chair like his life depends on it. It is like a punch through my heart.

It is him, but it isn't. He no longer looks like the rookie I met five years ago. The baby face is gone, replaced by a square jaw and sharp features. His blonde hair is combed back neatly out of his face and tucked behind his ears, brushing well past his shoulders, not like that first night when it was just long enough to cup each ear. It is now a full mass of waves reminding me of Brielle's hair when I pull a comb through her curls. He definitely put on that Pro weight. He is filling out his tailored suit in a way that would make any woman take a second look and a third.

His arms bulge against the suit's jacket, and his thighs stress his suit's pants. The black suit and crisp white shirt complement his tanned skin. The blue tie is the perfect finish, making him look like a perfectly wrapped package.

I don't have a thing for white men. I just have a thing for this white man. Five years and I cannot mistake the butterflies in my belly. There is no denying the fire I feel in my veins at the memory of his touch. I blink a few times and stumble back, reaching for my brother's hand and squeeze it hard.

"Oh my God," I gasp, "Oh my God, oh no, oh God no."

"I'll kill him," Ellerie growls beside me as his body tenses.

I snap out of it and turn to push at my brother's chest as he starts to launch himself toward Brad. I shake my head fiercely. This is not happening, it can't be.

"Listen to me Ellerie, he doesn't know, he didn't know. He never knew. I never even told him my name. It was one night. I was stupid and drunk, and Stacey had this idea not to tell him and his friend our names. I never tried to tell him. *Please,*" I whisper frantically trying to explain.

"You're kidding me right, Tam," Ellerie hisses. "You've known all this time who he was and where and you made us believe it was someone you didn't know how to find or contact."

"It's complicated. I was embarrassed. I was scared," I almost sob.

"Brad," Brielle squeals behind me.

I whip around to see him now standing less than a foot away. He is looking down at Brielle as a myriad of emotions cross his face. His large hand moves shakily toward her face, then drops back to his side. His hands clench then unclench.

His blue eyes mist over and then he squeezes them shut. He opens them and tries blinking a few times. The whole time Brielle stands staring up at him with a huge smile on her face.

His eyes slowly move up to meet mine and search my face. I watch his throat work as he swallows hard trying to find his words. One hand moves to run through his hair.

"I...is she...she's," he stammers out not able to complete a phrase. I nod, and he gulps down a breath of air.

This time, he reaches for my face and brushes my cheek. "Sweetheart, please tell me your name," he rasps.

"Tamara, Tamara Hathaway," I breathe.

His jaw works under his skin like he is trying my name out in his mouth. "Tamara," he drawls. "Tamara, we need to talk."

"I know," I murmur.

"Mommy," Brielle says looking at me with concern.

I reach for her, pulling her close, hugging her against me. Brad looks down at her and pain washes over his face. In that moment, I think that maybe I had made the wrong decision. Maybe he had a right to know about her.

"Bri, why don't you go with Uncle Eli, baby," I look down at her and say softly.

Brielle gasps and her face crumbles as her little bottom lip trembles. "Oh mommy, please don't be mad at Brad. I'm so sorry Brad, sorry Uncle Eli, I forgot it was supposed to be our secret," she sobs. She grabs Brad's hand and looks up at me. "Mommy, I ate first. Brad gave me food first. Please don't be mad at him. He's my new friend. I don't want him to get in trouble because I forgot."

"Bri, it's fine baby. He's not in trouble for giving you the cake. Just go with Uncle Eli," I soothe.

"But," she sniffles and looks up at Brad.

He squeezes her little hand in his and kneels down to her eye level. He brushes away a tear that slips free. It looks like he wants to cry with her.

"Sugar, it's okay. I need to talk to your mama. She's an old friend of mine. When we're done I'll come find you, and we can cause a little trouble with one of those go carts I saw them setting up," Brad says gruffly.

"You promise, you're not in trouble because of me, right," she pleads.

"I promise," he says and kisses her forehead.

"Okay," she whispers and throws her arms around his neck. She pulls away reluctantly, eyeing me warily as she walks over to Ellerie and takes his hand.

Ellerie gives Brad a curt nod, then squeezes my hand and gives me a tight smile. I know he is going to rip me a new one when he gets a chance. I watch them walk away, jumping when I feel a large hand settle on the small of my back.

"Can we take a walk somewhere private," he says next to my ear, causing my whole body to tingle. I nod and turn to follow him.

We make our way out of the tent and into the stadium. Brad leads me into the dark team locker room and flips the switch for the lights. I take a few steps forward to put a little distance between us.

Turning around I blurt out, "Brad, I'm so sorry. I didn't know what to do. I thought I would never see you again, and I didn't want to interrupt your life. You left, you didn't leave a way to contact you, so I thought it was best not to bother you."

He closes his eyes, and I can see his body vibrating. He stands like that for what seems like forever, but it is only a few seconds. When he opens his eyes, they are filled with tears, and his lashes are moist with them.

"Tamara, I'm so sorry. I left because I thought you would think that night was a mistake. We both had so much to drink and you….," he drops his head in his hands. "I've thought about you every day for five years. I have this picture I took of you with my phone while you were sleeping…I, I came back…it was a few months later but I went back, and you were gone. There was a man there with the realtor. I thought he looked something like you."

"My dad, he took care of selling my place when I moved here," I murmur.

He looks up at me and closes the distance between us cupping my face. "You've been here all this time, in Texas?" I nod, and he shakes his head, closing his eyes. "I'm so sorry.

She's mine, Brielle? She's really mine?" His voice holds so much awe.

"Yes," I whisper.

He shocks me when his big arms wrap around me and he lifts me from my feet spinning me in the air. His face buries into the crook of my neck as he squeezes me tight. He murmurs my name over and over, his laugh vibrating through my body as he holds me tight.

I wrap my arms around his neck not knowing what else to do. I am still unsure where this is going. I don't know if he will hate me for not telling him once the shock wears off. He still smells the same. I remember his cologne from crying over the pillow he slept on. It is like a blast from the past, citrusy and musky.

He slides me down his body, and I feel the evidence of his arousal press into my stomach. I can see the heat in his eyes as he looks down at my lips. I step back quickly surprised by his reaction to being close to me.

He clears his throat and looks into my eyes. "I want to be a part of her life, to get to know her," his brows draw together. "I missed four years. Please, I want to spend time with her."

I nod. "Sure, that's fine. I just want to take things slow, though. She can be sensitive as you can see. I don't know how she will take this. She is very smart, but this can be a little confusing."

"Okay, I understand. You have done such a good job with her. I'll do this your way, just tell me how," his eyes pierce mine as he speaks with sincerity.

Chapter 9

The last two weeks have been physically and emotionally exhausting. Between going back to work, Bri going back to day care, and Brad integrating into our lives, I am spent. There hasn't been a day when Brad hasn't been to my place.

Bri is beside herself with the idea that her new best friend comes to play with her every day. I didn't think it was possible for Brad to be in my house more than Ellerie, but he is. I have been cooking larger amounts of food because those two eat like each one of them is an entire football team by themselves.

I laughed when Brad told me that he was now on an organic diet. I supported my brother when he was conditioning for the game, so I have been eating organic for some years now. So Brad fits right in.

I can't seem to keep him off my mind. When I'm trying not to think of him Brielle is bringing him up with, 'Oh Mommy Brad said this,' or 'Oh Mommy Brad did that.' Sometimes I want to scream Bri please give Mommy a break with Brad. But when I see her little face light up, and I know she has no idea that she is talking about her father, it crushes me, and I let her talk all she wants.

It still doesn't help me to focus on anything other than him. We had a business lunch last week to talk about me representing him, and I spent most the time squirming in my seat. He makes those tailored suits look like the most delicious candy wrappers ever.

Here I am at a kiddy party, and I'm supposed to be taking pictures of my daughter, but my panties are soaked. I can't stop thinking about Brad in my back yard in a pair of swim trunks. Bri begged him to come over to swim with her yesterday, and he dropped everything to make her wish come true.

Oh, the man is sin on legs. His body is so ripped and huge. He was not that big or chiseled five years ago. Can feet be sexy? His are, I watched him padding around the pool wondering how that is possible. Then there is the hair. I would never have thought I would get used to it so long or like it, but it works on him. What doesn't?

He didn't have ink when I met him, but now he's covered in it. Tattoos were never my thing, but Brad is a canvas worth staring at. He has this intricate one on his chest over his heart that I couldn't make out without him catching me staring. The bicep of his right arm has a half sleeve with an amazing depiction of piano keys wrapping the arm under a timepiece, and a hand holding an Ace, King, Queen, and Jack of hearts. On his back and across his shoulder blades he has an angel rising out of a football field.

Whoever does his work is incredible. It was so cute when Bri asked him who drew on him and why'd he let them. Neither my brother nor I have any tats that Brielle has seen. Brad laughed really hard and told her he was stupid enough to let a friend draw on him, but her skin is too pretty to ever think about letting someone draw on her.

"Mommy, look how high I can jump," Brielle squeals drawing me back to the moment.

"Good job, baby," I beam and shift on my heels.

Ugh, I have on mile high heels at a kiddy party. I have to do something to get Brad's attention. He promised Brielle he would meet her here to meet her other friends. At first, he told her he would swing by after and pick her up to hang out with her. When I told him other adults would be here, including me, he was all for it. That's why I've been standing off to the side, further away from the other parents waiting for him.

The man has been driving me insane looking so good and forbidden. However, since I backed away from him in the locker room, he hasn't tried anything. He has asked if I am seeing anyone, using the excuse that he wanted to know if Brielle had any other father figures in her life other than Ellerie.

I was too chicken to ask him the same question. Instead, I have started to stalk my baby daddy on the internet. I know… it's sad. Supposedly, he recently broke up with some platinum blonde chick. She used to be a model or something. There haven't been any new pictures of them. I wonder if that is because he moved here or did they really break up like the rumors say.

I do catch him looking when he thinks I don't notice, so I'm hopeful. Then there is the way my body hums and the hairs on the back of my neck stand up whenever he is near me. Like when he is standing too close to look at something

111

over my shoulder, helping me dry the dishes or standing next to me to tuck Bri in at night, which he has stuck around to do all week.

Last night I was tied up preparing for meetings on Monday, and before I knew it I looked up and he had Bri fed, bathed and in her bed sound asleep. I was really grateful. The fact that he is so good with Bri is an extra turn on. He has adapted to calling her Ellie like Ellerie does. She loves it.

I'll be the first to admit it's not just his body I'm lusting after. I actually like Brad. He's funny, gentle and actually pretty smart. I hate to say I'm so surprised he is so smart. I guess I have to stop judging books by manufactured opinions because being white, country as hell and a jock does not add up to anything I had pictured in my mind.

It's easy to see he is young sometimes, but he is eager to learn and so patient with Brielle and even me. He didn't have to grow up as fast as I had to after having Brielle, but he is willing to now. So yeah, I have the hots for Brad for a number of reasons. In the last two weeks, I have wondered what more with him would be like.

So because I am too much of a coward to tell the father of my child that I think he is sexy, and I am completely turned on by him, I have resorted to dressing up for a kiddy party. One our daughter invited him to. I sigh as I shift on my heels again.

I look like I painted on my black skinny jeans, and my black t-shirt is snug across the breasts with a low V-neck. My four and a half inch grey suede heels have spikes on the heels. My shoes say anything but run around after children at a party.

I almost choked Brielle yesterday when she told Brad I went and got my hair done. She told him I never get my hair done unless I have an important event or her Auntie Alee is in town. She even went as far as telling him it wasn't Auntie Alee's time to visit.

Brad just gave me a smug smile and a wink. I didn't want to read too much into that. I haven't been with a man since I conceived my daughter. Well, not really, so I don't want to go miss reading his signals.

I do a little wiggle as my soaked panties start riding. This is so sad, but my vibrators are useless. They have never done it for me. I really think I am pathetic when the hairs on the back of my neck stand up, and my body starts humming.

This is happening with fantasies of him now too? *No!*

A heavy hand wraps around my hip and a hard chest leans against my back. I, at least, know I haven't completely lost my mind, although my panties are officially no good to me anymore.

"Hey Darlin'," his voice rumbles through me.

I look up at him and beam like a school girl. He drops a kiss to my forehead sending a shiver down my spine. I feel my skin flush and hope it isn't bright enough to show through my coloring.

"Hey," I breathe back.

"I got something special for my girls," he murmurs against my temple.

His girls, okay when did that happen? This man will be the death of me if I let him. I am panting like a wanton woman after just a few simple words. I don't even think I heard the words. It dawns on me that he is holding a gift bag up before my face.

"For me," I exhale.

"Yeah, Tamara for you," he chuckles. His eyes zone in on my lips, that I purposely painted with a natural color gloss that makes them look shiny, full and plump.

"Thank you," I say coyly, as I take the bag off his fingertips. I reach inside and pull out the golden box inside. I know what it is right away. I had told him about this place here that makes these posh cupcakes. I pop the top to the box and resting inside is my favorite, a yellow cake cupcake with buttercream frosting and gold covered chocolate shavings. "Brad, you didn't have to do this. This was so out of your way."

"Nothing is out of the way for my girls," he says with a broad grin.

There it is again, *my girls*. I look down at his hand on my waist, and he holds another smaller bag, which I know will have a mini version of my cupcake for Brielle. She is going to be on cloud nine.

He looks good enough to eat himself. What the man does for a suit is nothing compared to what he is doing for this black t-shirt and blue jeans. I wasn't expecting the tan construction boots, but that is Brad, never what I expect. I bite my bottom lip as my eyes rake over him. It is the first time I am seeing his heavy mass of hair tied back as well. Mmm, I might like him clean shaven, maybe.

"Brad," I start to say when I hear Brielle's cry crack through the room. I turn to find her, and she is barreling in our direction. I kneel so she can run into my arms, but she buzzes around me and runs right into Brad's arms.

He lifts her, cradling her little head against his neck as her body shakes with her tears. Brad rubs her back to soothe her as he kisses the top of her head. He looks in physical pain to see her upset. I close the distance when the shock of her rejection wears off and place my hand on her back beneath Brad's.

"Sugar, what's the matter," Brad coos. Brielle shakes her head and continues to sob. "Baby, come on now, what is it, you can tell me."

She lifts her head and sniffles. "Thomas called me a 'Bastward.' He said that's what I am because I don't have a daddy. He said my mommy wasn't pretty enough, and my daddy didn't love her or me enough to want us."

To say I am livid would be an understatement. I am pissed. Thomas has such nerve. To think he can't even say the damn word right. If he had Brielle sure would have pronounced it right. Brad's face goes from concerned to shocked, to absolute rage. In an instant, I know what he is going to do, and there is nothing I can do about it. I shove my hands in my hair trying to anchor myself for what is coming at me like a speeding bullet.

"Look at me, baby," Brad's voice rasps as he cups her little face and my eyes squeeze shut. "You are not a bastard. You have a daddy, and he loves you and your mommy very, very much. Your mommy is beautiful and so are you, baby."

"No, I don't have a daddy," Bri cries.

"Yes, you do baby," Brad chokes out.

No, no, no Brad. Don't do this, not now. I can't believe this is happening. Somewhere in the back of my mind, I am slowly processing he said he loved her and her mommy. I push that aside knowing he is just trying to console a three-year-old. I open my eyes and see the pain in his face. There is no way to stop him, and I am not sure if he is going to fix this or make it worse. He sweeps at her tears and ducks his head to look her in the eyes.

"That's not true. If I do where is he? Why isn't he here like Thomas's daddy," Brielle sobs.

"It is true." Brad presses his forehead to hers. "I'm right here, baby, I'm right here. I love you so much, Ellie. I promise you, baby, I love you. I didn't know. I would have been here, but I didn't know. I'll never leave you again."

Brielle's little mind is amazing. I knew it would take just a word, and she would know. She gasps and her head snaps back like his words are a slap. I hold my breath, not knowing what is coming. Her tiny hand goes to his face and cups his jaw.

"You're my daddy," she says in a little whisper.

"Yeah Ellie, I'm your daddy," Brad chokes, swallowing past a lump in his throat.

Brielle wraps her arms around his neck and squeezes so tight I don't think he can breathe. He is crushing her little body to him rocking from side to side. They stay like that for I don't know how long.

I want to break down and sob. This is my fault. I should have told him. I caused my baby so much pain, and I didn't even mean to. Brad looks up at me like he is reading my mind and reaches out to pull me into their hug.

"Let's go home," I say planting a kiss on Brielle's head. "Brad, can you take Ellie to the car. I'll take care of this."

He presses his lips and glares at me as realization for why this started comes back. I sigh and put my hands on my hips. He starts to say something, but I cut him off.

"Please Bradley, just take her outside. I'll handle it," I plead.

He doesn't look none too pleased, but he nods and bends to pick up the gift bag for Brielle, that he dropped when she charged into his arms. He looks at me long and hard like he is going to change his mind. Then backs away and turns to leave.

I turn and scan the room for Miranda. That Thomas is always up to something. I have no idea why any of the parents still bring their kids to his functions. I started to tell Brielle we weren't coming to this one, but she was so excited.

"Miranda, we need to talk," I bite out when I storm over to Thomas's mom.

"Hey Tam, what is it Sugar," Miranda says with a smile until she looks up at my face.

"It's Thomas; he just said some things to Bri that I don't appreciate," I say then tell her what Brielle told us.

Miranda turns beet red, and her jaw flaps like a fish as she tries to find words. I drop my hip and put my fists on my waist. I raise my brow, waiting impatiently for her to get her crap together.

"Tam, I …" she stammers.

"What's going on Miranda?" Perry, Miranda's husband drawls.

"Thomas," she growls. "H-he called Bri a bastard and said her mama ain't pretty enough to keep her daddy around. Now where would he get something like that from Perry?" Miranda is now fuming at her husband.

Perry snorts as his beady little eyes rake over me. He licks his lips and gives me a smug smile. He is the bastard; he's asked me to sleep with him more than once.

My body starts that humming and the hairs on my neck are at attention. I groan internally. Brad's hand splays my belly possessively and draws me back against his chest.

I crane my neck. "I thought I asked you to take Ellie to the car," I murmur.

"I did but she forgot her shoes, we had to come back," he explains then looks up at Miranda and Perry.

Perry's mouth is gaping open as he looks at Brad. Then his eyes flicker between Brad and Brielle in his arms, several times before bouncing to me. Perry swallows, then draws a hand over his face. I turn into Brad's side and sink into his warmth, and his arm tightens around me. He looks down at me to search my face, then plants a kiss on my forehead.

"Bradley Monroe," Perry says sounding puzzled and holding out his hand. Brad nods, takes his hand and squeezes harder than he has to. "C-can we get you something? My boy would love to meet you. It's his birthday party."

"We're actually leaving. I don't take too kindly to folks making my baby cry. Maybe I'll meet your boy at Brielle's princess party when he comes to show he has better manners," Brad says matter-of-factly.

"I'm sorry about the kid. He can be a real little shit sometimes," Perry says like a goofball.

"Oh my God, I'm so embarrassed," Miranda groans. "Bradley, Tam, I apologize for my entire family. Thomas will be dealt with, and again, I am so sorry."

"Y'all have a good night. Let's go Darlin'," Brad says and tugs me toward the door.

"Can I ride with Daddy, Mommy, please," Bri whines.

"Sweetie, your seat is in my car, he'll be right behind us," I tell her.

"*Please*," Bri whines.

"How about this Sugar, I'll strap you in your seat, and you'll ride with your mama. I'll follow you in my car, and when we get to your house, I'll give you a ride on my back all the way into the house," Brad says with a big smile.

"Okay," Brielle beams. She throws her arms around his neck and kisses his cheek. "I love you, Daddy."

"I love you too, Ellie. So much," Brad chokes.

We reach my car. Unlocking it and opening the back door, Brad places Brielle in her seat and straps her in, as I make my way around and into the driver's seat. He whispers something in Brielle's ear, and she squeals with laughter. When he tickles her, I watch her face glow and my heart aches. She fell in love with Brad from the moment she met him. It was like she knew who he was all along.

"Daddy, can we have pizza when we get home," Brielle chirps.

Brad throws his head back and laughs. "You be a good girl for your mama on the way home, and we'll see if we can work some magic on her," he says and winks at her.

"I'll be good, promise," she coos.

"I have no doubts, Sugar," he says with a broad grin and ducks to kiss her on the head.

He closes her door then walks around my truck and taps my window. I press the button and the window slides down. Without warning, he cups the back of my neck and ducks his head in the car crushing my lips with his. It isn't an open mouth kiss. It is a promise of more to come.

"Drive safe," he murmurs against my lips. He backs away from the truck. I start it and back out of the space. I look in my rearview as I exit the parking lot to see him watching our safe departure before walking to jump into his truck to follow.

Chapter 10

Watching Brielle with her father tonight, tore at my heart. She missed out on so much because of me. My poor choices hurt her and Brad. She needs her father more than anything. That's why I know what I have to do. I can't be with him and mess things up. Brielle needs her father in her life more than I need a man in my bed.

They looked so happy together. She fought sleep as long as she could, trying to stay up to play with him. It's like she thought he would disappear if she went to sleep. That's what made my decision, the thought that she fears he will disappear.

Brad just took her upstairs to put her in bed, and I plan to talk to him tonight. We haven't kissed or anything since we got back to the house, though his hands would find my waist on occasion. It would just be better this way.

Just as I convince myself, I am doing the right thing, I bend over to pick up Brielle's things from the couch. Brad's hands cradle my waist, and he steps up behind me. I straighten, and he pulls me flush against him nudging my hair aside with his face and planting wet kisses to my neck.

"Brad," I moan. "We ne –," I start, but he cuts me off. Pulling my face to his and capturing my lips.

I forget what I am trying to say and turn to face him. He deepens the kiss slipping his tongue into my mouth. He groans and tips my head back.

Brielle, she's more important. I pull away and put distance between us. Brad's brows draw together. He runs his hands through his hair.

He looks so good. His shirt is untucked from his jeans, and his feet are bare. His hair is even loose again. He looks like he made himself right at home. I touch my tingling lips, trying to focus and figure out how to do this. He pinches the bridge of his nose, then lets his eyes roam over me. His eyes narrow on my face and in that moment he decides something.

Like lightning, he shoots at me closing the distance and crushing my mouth with his once again. Brad's hands lock in my hair, holding me in place. I push up on my toes and wrap my arms around his neck moaning into his mouth. His hand slides out my hair, down my body, and cups my butt.

"Tamara," He groans and squeezes. Next thing I know, he is lifting me up and wrapping my legs around his waist.

Never breaking the kiss, he starts for the stairs. I am lost in his cologne, in his taste. His kisses are hungry and almost desperate. He takes us upstairs to my bedroom, pushing the door closed behind us with his back. When the door clicks closed some of my sense clicks back in place with it.

"Brad," I pant. "We shouldn't do this."

"Tam, baby just let me love on you. I know you want this as much as I do. Let me please you, baby," Brad groans.

"Brad," I try again, but he nips at my bottom lip before dropping me onto the bed and coming down to hover over me.

I give up when his mouth wraps around my breast through my shirt. I cry out and Brad groans. Soon clothes are flying everywhere. Brad cups my face and drinks from my lips with soft kisses. When I feel him start to push into me, I freak out and push at his chest.

"Brad, condom," I pant.

"You can't be serious," he groans pushing forward again.

"I'm very serious Brad. I'm not on birth control. I'm allergic to it. That's how I got pregnant with Bri," I explain.

"Really?" He smirks down at me and nudges my soaked entrance a little more. "I want a son, Tamara."

"Are you crazy? I've in all seriousness known you for two weeks and a night. Not to mention I have no clue what you have been doing in the last five years. Thank God Bri was all you gave me the first time. No glove, no love Brad. I mean it."

He growls and gives me a chaste kiss on the mouth before rolling off me and standing. He walks over to the pile of our clothes and fishes around for his jeans retrieving a condom from his wallet. Even his ass is hot; *someone help me.*

He turns to watch me, grinning as he rolls the condom on while making his way back onto the bed. He looks so sexy with his blonde hair disheveled and spilling over his shoulders. He scoops me into his arms, kissing me long and deep. He sinks into me nice and slow.

"Tamara, I'm going to make you fall in love with me and then I'm putting my son in your belly," he growls.

"Mmm, Brad shut up. I missed you," I moan.

"I missed you too, Baby."

Oh, how have I gone this long without this? He even feels larger than the last time. I pull my knees back to my chest needing to feel as much of him as I can. Bradley doesn't disappoint as usual. He starts to drive into me deeper groaning as his eyes roll back into his head.

"Oh my God, baby," he growls loudly. "You feel so good."

"You do too," I whimper. "Babe, you're so hard, you feel so good."

"I'm so hard for you. I've dreamt a million times of being back inside you."

"Ah," I moan.

I almost purr when his hair spills forward between us. It is tickling my breasts and creating an unexpected sensation as our bodies become slick with our sweat. I slide my fingers down his back and squeeze his tight backside.

Brad takes the queue and starts to really pound into me. His full lips fuse to mine, and I know I'm going to explode. He knows it too as he lifts my hips off the bed and plows into me.

"Brad," I whisper scream because it is so good my voice leaves me.

"Tamara," he bellows back before collapsing against me. He catches his breath, then looks me in the eyes. "I'm going to need more condoms."

I just laugh and shake my head at him.

~B~

I stare up at the ceiling thinking about how this turned into the perfect day. I spent the morning with my mom and dad. I couldn't stop talking about Ellie. They are so excited to meet her. I know Tamara wants to take things slow. My mom says she's right, and I'm trying, I really am, but I want my family so bad. That's what Tamara and Ellie are; they're my family.

When my baby girl looked at me and told me, she loved me my heart almost burst open. I love that little girl so much.

129

She's so beautiful and smart just like her mama. I wasn't joking when I told Tam I want a son. I want to watch her grow with my baby inside her this time. I want to be there for all the stuff I missed with Ellie.

My mama told me to give Tamara time, to keep my hands off her until she is ready. I had planned on waiting, at least, two months before trying to have sex with her. But when I walked into that place for that birthday party and saw her wiggling in those skin tight jeans, I lost my mind. I wanted to throw her over my shoulder and run out to my truck with her.

It took everything I had in me to wait until tonight. When she started to reject me tonight, my old insecurities tried to creep in. I thought she was saying no because of the race thing, but when I looked into her eyes, I saw it. I saw how badly she wanted me too. I hadn't misread the looks she's been giving me.

I want her to get to know me and me to get to know her. I want her to know I'm not leaving again. I know we can make this work. She's the one. I look over at her and smile.

Tamara is so beautiful when she sleeps. I try to let her sleep. I really do, but for five years I have been waiting for this. I watch my fingers glide up her arm and over that shoulder I know so well. I'm hard as a rock and looking at her and touching her isn't helping. My baby sleeps like the dead. I've made so much noise hoping she'd wake up, and I wouldn't have to feel bad about waking her. *Forget that.*

Smack.

"Ouch," Tamara yelps and shifts in the bed rubbing her ass where I just smacked it. I chuckle and brush her hand out of the way to rub it for her. "Brad, what's wrong with you," she grumbles.

"Baby, I went to the store for those condoms an hour and a half ago," I complain.

"Boy, if you don't take your country ass to sleep," she hisses then starts giggling when I nip her ear and tickle her ribs.

"My country what," I chuckle and nip her shoulder.

She gasps when I slide my hand between her legs. "Brad," she moans.

"I've wanted to hear you say my name for five years, Tamara," I groan. "Your body is tighter than I remember. How many have been in here after me?"

"No one," she cries out throwing her head back against my shoulder.

I grin with satisfaction. "No one, Darlin'."

"No, no one," she sucks in a breath. "M-my…oh Brad, my vibrator…oh…but it never feels like this, like you so…ah…I…I stopped try…ing. Brad, Brad, Brad."

I nudge my way in from behind after quickly suiting up. She is killing me with those moans and calling my name. Knowing she hasn't been with anyone else drives me mental. I need to claim her. I'm so in love with her.

"You're mine, Tamara," I growl as I give her all of me. "I want you to be mine. You're all I want, you. I want my family Tamara. *Mine.*"

I don't mean to go all caveman and lose my head but with this woman, this is who I am. I need to have her, need to protect her, need to make her happy. I break when she whimpers and throws her arms back, locking them around my neck. My eyes lock on her breasts bouncing as I drill into her. I can't hold anything back anymore. I make love to her like my life depends on it.

Chapter 11

I feel soft kisses raining across my forearm and stir. I yawn, blinking a couple of times to realize I'm lying on a big hard body. My face is in his chest, and my arm must have been shoved in his face from the angle it is at.

I lift my head and peek up at him. He smiles grabbing my sides and sliding me up his body to kiss my nose then nuzzling my neck. *Someone tell this man I am thirty, not eighteen.*

"Bradley, seriously," I giggle when he cups my butt and grinds me into his erection.

"You said Ellie won't come looking for you until noon. We have a half hour," he murmurs into my neck.

"Babe, give me some time to recuperate. You wore it out last night," I whine. "And let me brush my teeth."

Bradley's chest rumbles with laughter as I push up and roll out of bed, heading for the bathroom. I use the bathroom and wash my hands, then slap some water on my face. I look myself over as I brush my teeth. I am glowing. I am so happy. I am happy until I notice the biggest bite mark ever on my neck.

I spit the toothpaste out and rinse my mouth. "I'm gonna kill him," I growl.

I run into the room and jump on him, straddling his sides and wrap my fingers around his thick neck. He is startled at first but starts laughing at my feeble attempt. I growl in frustration, and he flips me onto my back, hovering his huge frame over me.

"What," he chuckles and nips my lower lip.

"What, are you fifteen? Why in the hell do you have to leave hickeys all over me," I snap. "How the hell do you even manage to get them everywhere without me noticing, I look like I have eggplant patches all over me?"

"I think my marks are sexy on you. They say you belong to me," he retorts smugly.

"They're humiliating, Brad. Last time I didn't even know I had them and my mother was the one that pointed them out," I whine.

"Oh Darlin', I'm sorry," he snickers. I slip my hand free and slap him upside the head. "No Tam, I'm sorry, Darlin'. Let me take you and my little girl shopping today. I'll get you something really pretty so you can cover it up."

"I don't know. I think you should go home and be alone to think about what you've done," I pout.

"I've been alone long enough Sweetheart. Now, you going to let me spoil my girls today or are we going to stay in bed all day so I can show you how lonely I've been."

"Brad," I moan as he snakes his hand between my legs.

"I love that sound."

"Babe, we can't. Ellie won't come bother me until noon, but she is still up. She'll hear us," I whimper as his tongue flicks over the sensitive skin on my neck.

He sighs and rolls off of me with a heavy thump on the bed. He untangles the sheets and pulls me back on his chest before covering us both. I kiss his chest then take the time to really look at that tat that has me so curious. I gasp and sit up holding the sheet to my chest.

"Brad, that's me," I point to his chest. I look up at the smile on his face then bend over his chest to look again. It is so realistic; it looks like a black and white photo has been screen-printed to his chest. You can see the detailing of Brad's head raised as he looks down at me lying on his chest. You can make out the side of my face and my shoulder and the sheet fans out just below my shoulder blades.

"Babe," I question with my brows drawn.

"I told you I had a picture of you. I've never stopped thinking about you, Tam." He brushes his fingers across my cheek. "I wanted you as close to my heart as I could get you. I needed to fill the hole losing you left."

"Bradley," I say in almost a whisper. "You meant what you said yesterday didn't you?"

"What, that I want a son? As soon as you're ready, yup," he says wiggling his brows at me.

"No silly, you told Ellie you love her and her mommy very, very much," I say coyly.

Brad sits up and cups my face. "I fell in love with you the very first time I laid eyes on you. I've been in love with you ever since. Yes, Tamara, I love you."

I take his hand in mine and squeeze it. I give him the most serious look I can muster. "Bradley, my big country giant, I'm going to make you work a whole lot harder than that to get those words out of my mouth." I burst out laughing when he groans.

"At least, I know what I'm dealing with because I really want that son," he chuckles.

"You have a one track mind, geesh."

He throws his head back and laughs. Wrapping an arm around my shoulders, he pulls me back down with him. He kisses the top of my head.

"Can I ask you something else?"

"Anything."

"Have you been with a lot of women since me?"

"You really want me to answer that?"

I look up at him, and he looks amused. I sigh and shrug. "I guess not. But how did other women take it to see me resting on your chest?"

"Darlin', I wasn't with many women. The one relationship I tried to have," he sighs heavily. "This tat started a lot of shit. She was jealous anyway, I think, but seeing the tat caused a lot of trouble. She was never right for me in the first place. To be honest, the tat broke us up. She gave me an ultimatum to have it covered or removed and give her a more solid commitment or she was leaving. I had her shit packed for her and shipped to her place."

"Remind me not to give you ultimatums," I tease.

"Baby, anything you ask for I'll give you. You don't have to worry about that."

"Did you love her?"

"Who?"

"The girl you were in the relationship with."

"Tiffany, no I never loved her. I felt so lost for so long. She was a friend for a while before we dated. It started out as innocent flirting and a few dates. Then she wanted to get more serious so she showed up at a road game after a win and we made things physical. It was about a month after that that she actually saw the tattoo.

"I wasn't really hiding it. I just knew her and knew it would cause a problem. One night she forced her way into sleeping over, and she saw it when I came out the shower. She went nuts at first.

"I hadn't known that she saw the picture beforehand when looking through some of my things. She said I was still seeing you, and that's why I was so distant. She called me cold, said I had to be to have another woman on my chest while I was in her. I guess she was right. But I warned her in the beginning that she was not getting all of me because I knew I belonged to someone else. She pushed anyway."

"You do know I'm not inking your face anywhere on my body," I snort.

"Oh yeah," he chuckles and starts tickling me, "how about here...or here...or maybe here."

"Brad stop," I gasp for air as I laugh.

Like clockwork the door bursts open and Brielle comes bouncing in the room. I bite back my laughter and curse under my breath. I didn't realize we were lying here so long. I am still butt naked. Brad only has on his boxers, which he must have put on when I was in the bathroom.

"Daddy," Brielle squeals. She bounces up on the bed and launches herself at him, wrapping her arms around his neck.

He gives me a wink to let me know he will keep her distracted. I edge to the side of the bed where I spot his t-shirt from yesterday. I snatch it up and slip it on quickly. Brad is holding her head away from me and whispering in her ear while he tickles her.

She squeals with laughter. "Daddy, you're so silly," she squeals. "Mommy's not going to make us eat candy for breakfast. She'll make us pancakes, right Mommy?"

"It's lunchtime, and I think I'm going to leave you two to fin for yourselves. You are both too happy and loud for a quiet Sunday morning," I tease.

"Please can we have pancakes," Brad says with a pout as he holds Brielle in his arms with her back to his chest. She cranes her neck to see his pout then gives one of her own.

"You have got to be kidding me," I say to the almost identical faces.

"Please," Brad whines.

"Ugh, go home."

"Home is where the heart is, Darlin'."

I lean in and place my hand over the tattoo over his heart. "Just so you know I just might be falling too," I whisper against his lips as I kiss him.

Chapter 12

It's mid-April in Texas, and I am wearing a damn scarf around my neck. True to his word Brad took us shopping yesterday to make up for the bite marks he left on my neck, but that does not make me any less annoyed that I have to wear this stupid thing. Bad enough I felt like I was choking in the lightweight turtleneck I had to wear yesterday, now I have this little scarf on looking like a flight attendant.

Brad was happy with his purchase of a fresh t-shirt and jeans to change into. Then it was off to spoil me and Brielle, which he thoroughly did. He bought me, at least, a week's worth of these scarves and a few high-necked blouses to wear until the marks fade. He also bought me a few dresses I had my eye on, a pair of shoes that were more for his benefit and a charm bracelet, I insisted I didn't need.

Then there were the short shorts he bought for his eyes only to go with the shoes he had to buy. According to him, the shorts are for when we play Dukes of Hazzard. I got a good laugh out of that. We did a lot of laughing yesterday, unlike this morning. We did nothing but fight this morning, which should have been an indicator that today was going to be a crap day.

It started with me catching him using my toothbrush and flipping out. He feels just because his tongue knows every inch of my body intimately that it shouldn't matter if he borrows my toothbrush. I think that is more of a reason it should.

The next fight started when he decided he wanted to shower with me and then decided a shower wasn't all he wanted. I was down with the extra until he pulled me under the spray of the water wetting my hair. He didn't get that I was trying to stop him until it was too late. So instead of getting Brielle dressed I had to dry my hair, which caused our next three arguments.

He wanted to help, so he went to get Brielle ready for school. Brielle is a very smart little girl, but she is not to be trusted picking her own outfit. Which Brad just happened to let her do. I came down to breakfast, and my baby looked like she was going to the circus as a clown princess.

Brad just thinks anything she does is adorable and couldn't see why I was yet again freaking out. I had to skip breakfast to get her into a new outfit, which caused her and me to fight. Because her daddy said, she looked pretty in her outfit.

Which would lead me to the spoiling Brad did with Bri yesterday. He bought her anything she squealed about and then some, including a pair of one and a half carat earrings. He wanted to buy her larger ones, but I only won the argument because the bigger ones really didn't look good in her tiny ears.

Then there are the diamond butterfly hair clips he insisted on buying her. I mean I understand he feels he missed out on so much with her and wants to make up for it. I also understand he is single and has more money than he knows what to do with. He can more than afford to spoil us. But really, diamond hair pins... come on dude.

So of course, mommy was the bad guy when she made Brielle, daddy's little princess, change into a pair of capris, a tank top, and flat shoes. Plus, I refused to let her, at least, wear the hair pins. Brielle threw a full out tantrum. I needed to be out the door getting to the office, to get ready for several morning meetings. Brad understood why I told Brielle no but still wanted to cave because of the tears.

At that point, I was pissed and told him sleepovers were over. If Brielle wasn't staring in his mouth, that argument would have been a lot worse. Brad has every intention of being in my house as much as he can and has said so more than once.

Our last argument happened when Ellerie showed up, as usual, to take Brielle to school. I needed to be out the door, and things are usually always so smooth in the mornings. Ellerie is used to grabbing Brielle and being on their way. Having Brad there threw everyone off. Brielle wanted Brad to take her, but Brad doesn't know the routine and the school has no clue who he is to her.

Brad was annoyed that I didn't tell Ellerie that he didn't have to take Brielle and let him do it instead. So twenty minutes after Bri and Ellerie were gone, and thirty after I should have been out of the door, I was still standing in the kitchen fussing with Brad. He eventually caved and apologized asking me to be more patient with him and the situation. I gave in too and teased him.

"I don't think I have enough patience to teach my white boy what not to do with a black woman's hair," I snort.

"Ha, but you did just say *your* white boy. That's all that matters Darlin', I promise I'll figure out the rest," he says with a heartbreaking smile.

He reached out for me, and I slapped his hand away. "Oh no Brad, I needed to leave a long time ago. I'll see you later," I pushed up on my toes and pecked his lips.

"I love you, Darlin', and I am sleeping over tonight," he crooned with a boyish grin.

"Perv," I teased and rushed him out of the door.

If only the drama and frustration ended there, but for me, life is never that simple. That is why I am now heading to my boss's office upon his request to see me as soon as I got in. Thank God I am only late according to my standards. I usually come in early every day to get ahead of my tasks so today it is like I am here on time with everyone else.

I know this is not a social visit. Cyrus Pierson will come see you if it is a friendly visit. When you are getting chewed out, he wants you on his territory. I think it is his huge desk and chair he sits in that he likes to use to anchor fear in his subjects. I haven't been summoned into Pierson's office since I got hired. He always stops by my office.

I stop outside his office door to straighten my suit jacket and smooth my hands over my pencil skirt. I finger my sweeping bangs and my bun before reaching to knock, then pushing open the door.

"Ah Tamara, come have a seat dear," Cyrus drawls. It's funny Ellerie, and I are probably the only people in this state that don't have a drawl even after five years. Even Brielle sounds more like she is from Texas than the daughter of a New Yorker. Cyrus is sitting behind his desk with his fingers steepled in front of his mouth. His lips are pinched, a sure tell that he is pissed about something.

I walk to one of the chairs in front of his desk with confidence and sit gracefully. Cyrus leans forward, picking up the newspaper from his desk and tosses it toward me. He raises a brow, drawing to his full height in his seat and glares.

"I was a little disappointed you haven't confided in me about Monroe," he gripes, his face transforming to a look of hurt.

How does he know about Brad? My brows draw together, and I reach for the paper he tossed at me. Right on the front page is a picture of Brad with Brielle cradled in one arm at his hip, and me tucked under the other arm while shopping bags hung from his hands. He is wearing his shades, and his face is turned up at Brielle. He is kissing her cheek while her head is thrown back in laughter. I am looking up at both of them with a face splitting grin of my own.

I suck in a deep breath and groan. The headline reads, *The Reason Texas Son Returns*, with smaller caption reading, *Is He Back for Love?* This cannot be my life. I told Brad we needed to move slowly; this is not slow. Two weeks and now my life is a front page story and boy, are they wrong. I flip through to the story in the paper, and there are several more pictures.

Brad with his arm locked around my waist, staring down at me. One with Brad kissing me senseless, another with Brad feeding Brielle his frozen yogurt, they even had a freaking picture of Brad purchasing Brielle's earrings and hair pins. There are two pages worth of pictures of us plastered across them.

I mentally curse pinching my eyes closed to try to think. Something I should have done yesterday. I should have known better. Brad's leaving California and coming to Texas is huge. No one expected it. They are craving a juicy story to go with it.

"Cyrus, our relationship is complicated," I start, but he gives me a *do-I-look-like-I-care* look, cutting off my explanation. I quickly change my approach. "We had a business meeting last week I have just been giving him time to consider my proposal. I should have confirmation no later than the end of this week."

"While this is a big account for the firm Tam, that is not my main concern. When your father called in the favor for me to hire you on, I saw it as my duty to a friend. I see you as a daughter, whether you know it or not." Cyrus sighs. "You're one of the best we have; I have no doubts you'll bring Monroe onto your roster. What I am concerned with is if you know what you are getting yourself into here."

I bristle a little. "What do you mean?"

"I mean this is Texas honey, I am going to speak frankly here. The boys that run the league won't be too happy about their star player having a black woman on his arm. No matter how beautiful you are," Cyrus says with a grimace and fidgets with his tie.

My head whips back as if he just slapped me. I open my mouth ready to let him have it. Good friend of my father's or not. Cyrus lifts his hand to stop me and continues.

"Now I see the wheels turning in your head. You have known me for years now, Tam. I have never treated you as anything less than a great attorney or one of my very own daughters. So reel the anger in," he gives me a stern look. "I've been around a long time. I watched many of my friends, including your father fight their way through a lot of doors. They have paved a way for amazing minds like yours. What concerns me Tamara is that the League looks the other way for many things but this… Does your father know? How does he feel?"

I take a minute to really take my boss in. He looks truly concerned and sincere. Cyrus has always been warm with me, but I have never seen him show so much emotion. With a nod to myself, I answer.

"My dad doesn't know about Brad or the details of our relationship. Things are complicated and sort of new," I say trying not to fidget.

Cyrus lifts a brow and gives me a look that says, *"it doesn't look so new to me."* Yeah, I'm so not getting into this with my boss and one of my dad's buddies. I already know that I owe my dad a call before this all gets out of hand.

"Your father has a right to be proud of you. I'm glad he sent you our way. However, after seeing these pictures, I want to make sure that we are protecting your best interests. I have watched you work too hard to see anyone try to take that from you.

"I have seen what this type of situation can lead to," Cyrus pauses as a grim look crosses his face. I couldn't help but wonder what this man isn't telling me. It is clear that his mind has drifted for a moment. "Is this something you really want? Is this a serious relationship? I ask not to get in your business Tamara, but because I want to be prepared on all accounts when this can of worms bursts."

"Sir, like I said it is complicated, and I'm not sure where things are leading. Brad and I have a history that links us together and presents the desire for more on both our behalves. We are just trying to take things slow," I start.

Cyrus throws his head back in a deep throaty laugh. "Dear, taking things slow went out the window with the snap of the first photo," Cyrus says with amusement in his voice and on his face.

I rub at my forehead, trying to ease the headache coming on. I groan and try to wrap my head around what is happening. How can such a wonderful day turn into this? Yesterday I had thoughts of what it would be like if we were a real family. Bri was just so happy. I have to admit so was I. Now it just seems like we are piling mistake on top of mistake.

"Listen, Tamara," Cyrus sighs. "I want you to know I am in support of whatever you decide to do here. Just know that I am in your corner. It will be better for you to remember you have people in your corner that care and will be there."

I wrinkle my nose not at his words, but at the unusual display of emotions coming forth in his words. "Thank you," is the only thing I can think to say. I have known my boss for longer than I have worked here, and I have never known him to show emotions so easily. Just like that, his mask slips back into place.

"Your father has informed me he will be in town soon. He has agreed to join me at the country club for some golf. I believe Bradley should join us," Cyrus says with more of a smile. I just stare at the old man with his brown hair greying at the temples. He is in his mid-fifties and still running things with an iron fist. His olive skin has faired the years pretty well, better than his ex-wife's.

I guess that's why he divorced and married a younger woman. Rumor has it that he was actually married a third time, but no one speaks of it with any true knowledge or detail. I have always thought of him as a little mysterious.

"I don't know if Brad plays," I start then sigh, this is not a suggestion it is a demand. I laugh to myself as I realize how much this man has been like a father and a mentor over the last five years. "I'll let Brad know, and I'll have Daddy let him know when to join you both."

"If this is the path you decide to choose," Cyrus says tapping a finger on the paper. "It won't be easy, but it can work for you in many ways, Tamara. I am here to make sure it does. It looks like you're now in a steady, stable relationship. That family of yours and this magnitude of client will land you in that partner seat dear," Cyrus changes directions a bit with talk of partnership, to my relief the air in the room changes.

I am annoyed that he is implying I need to be attached to make partner, but I know it is a part of the game. It is one of the reasons I had tried dating Mike. He plays basketball here in Texas and is a friend of Ellerie's. We have some mutual friends back home as well. He would have liked for things to go further, but I just couldn't give the relationship what it needed.

As I try to figure out my jumbled feelings and thoughts, a knock comes at the door, which is odd. Cyrus assistant Melanie is efficient she would have buzzed to inform Cyrus of another guest.

"Come in," Cyrus's voice cracks through the room.

"Excuse me Mr. Pierson, Miss. Hathaway," my assistant, says as she rushes into the room holding my cell phone. "I know you said hold your calls, but it is Brielle's day care there is an emergency."

I jump from my seat and grab the phone, forgetting everything else including where I am. "Hello," I rush into the phone when I take it off mute.

"Hi Tamara, this is Cynthia. Um, we had a bit of an incident this morning," the coordinator of Brielle's day care says into the phone. "The children were in the yard for morning activities, and there were tons of photographers and reporters outside the playground gates. They were screaming for Brielle and calling out questions to her and the staff. Brielle is still pretty upset, and the reporters are still milling around the area. I think maybe it would be best if you come to get her."

I can hear the nerves in Cynthia's voice. My brain is racing. This day is trying to kill me. I have to act fast.

"Oh my God, is she okay," I ask with concern.

"She is shaken up, but physically okay."

"Cynthia, I have to be in a meeting in the next hour. My brother has a mandatory training and therapy session scheduled today. Stacey is out of town," I am really thinking out loud. "Listen, I can see if her father can come. He is not on the emergency contact card, but I can fax your permission to release her to him if that will work."

"Under these circumstances, you can just give me a name and he will need to have ID for us to photocopy. He can then just sign her out," Cynthia replies.

"His name is Bradley Monroe," I say.

I hear her suck in a breath on the other end and go completely quiet. I don't have time for this. Cynthia is the epitome of star-struck when it comes to celebrities. She still can't pull it together when Ellerie or Stacey go to the school for anything.

"Breathe Cynthia," I snap.

"Sorry Tamara," she breathes.

"I'll call Brad to see if he can get there. If he can, my assistant will call you back to confirm, if anything changes call right away. If he can't come, I will figure things out and get back to you myself," I ramble.

"Okay," Cynthia replies, and I end the call dialing Brad right away.

I still hadn't taken note of the fact that I am pacing my boss's office. All I know is my baby needs to be protected. Someone needs to get to her. *Please answer Brad, please answer.*

"Hey Darlin'," Brad answers the phone. "I thought you would be in your meeting by now."

"Brad it's Bri," I rush. "Reporters and photographers are all over her school. Did you see the paper yet? There are so many pictures of us from yesterday. Babe, I need you to get to Bri. Her daycare wants someone to pick her up, and I can't get there and back in time."

"Shit," Brad growls. I can hear weights clinking in the background. "Calm down, Baby. I'll take care of it. I just found out about the pictures before you called. Sorry Tam, I should have seen this, I'll fix it, I promise."

"Okay, I'll text you the address of the day care. You need to have your ID, and you'll have to sign her out. Babe, she is upset."

"I'm already halfway to my truck, Tam," Brad reassures me.

"Okay, I'm hanging up to text you."

"I love you, Baby."

"I know. Please text me as soon as she is safe."

I cut the call and text the address right away. I stop pacing and whip around to face my assistant ready to do damage control. Reality is setting back in.

"Maryann, call the day care back and let them know Brad is on the way. Screen my calls, if the daycare calls forward those to Bradley Monroe. His number is in my phone. When the papers start calling, I have absolutely no comment. And Maryann, forget everything you just heard in this room," I say sternly.

"Yes, Miss. Hathaway," Maryann nods.

I straighten my jacket and go to take my seat again as if nothing happened. Cyrus raises a brow at me then chuckles and sits back in his seat. "You always think on your toes Tamara. It's what makes you great at what you do. Don't lose that. I think we are done here."

"Thank you."

Chapter 13

I punch the roof of my truck when I pull into a parking space in front of the daycare. I can see the vultures surrounding the place. I called my security team and had them rush right over to make sure no one tried to get to Ellie. My one job is to keep my girls safe and happy.

Right now I suck at both. Tamara is pissed at me right now for more reasons than I can count. Now I've let them both down by not thinking about what our little shopping trip would do. Being back home and being with my girls has me feeling like myself so much that I forgot all about being a football star.

I can't blame Tamara for not saying she loves me back. I haven't shown her that I have a right to her love. I keep messing things up.

I rushed out of the weight room as soon as Tamara told me what was going on. I didn't stop to shower or change. Meaning I'm pissed, I smell, and I have on workout gear. I never thought I could be more pissed than when my baby cried in my arms because that little snot nose kid called her a name. This tops that ten times over.

I tug on my baseball cap and throw on a pair of shades and jump out of my truck. When my security guys spot me, they rush to usher me into the school. When we step inside, there is a little redhead standing in front of the receptionist desk. She is patting her hair and fidgeting with her clothes.

"Hello, Mr. Monroe. I'm Daly Cynthia," she blushes ten shades of red. Her eyes pinch shut, and she brushes her hands down the sides of her jeans. She clears her throat and holds her hand out. "Excuse me; I'm Cynthia Daly, the program coordinator. I have Brielle in my office with one of the teacher's assistants. She is still quite upset."

It is clear that she is nervous and possibly a fan, but I need to get to my little girl. I nod at her curtly, and she turns on her heels to lead the way to her office. When she opens the door, I spot Ellie right away in the arms of a woman that is trying hard to soothe her with no success. Ellie peeks up

160

through her tear soaked lashes and jumps from the woman's arms.

I catch her as she leaps in the air toward me locking her in my arms where I know she is safe. Her little body is shaking in my arms, tearing at my heart. Her little sobs are destroying me.

"Daddy, I'm so happy you're here. I was so scared," Ellie sobs.

"It's okay, Sugar. You're safe now," I murmur as I kiss her head repeatedly.

"I want to go home."

"First, you have to do daddy a favor and quit all this crying. Then we can go home and sneak some chocolate ice cream. That'll get that pretty little smile back on my baby's face, won't it," I ask looking into those eyes that are so much like mine.

"Can I have sprinkles?"

"We'll see," A laugh rumbles in my chest.

I pull my wallet from my pocket and hand over my ID to the nervous redhead, who is watching Ellie and me with wide eyes. She snaps out of it and takes the ID, rushing out of the room. She is back a moment later with a photocopy in one hand and my ID in the other. I take the ID back placing it back into my wallet.

"Is there anything else," I ask.

She swallows nervously and nods her head, waving me to follow her. We walk back to the reception desk where she retrieves a white binder from the receptionist. She scribbles in some information then turns the book to me.

"Please sign here."

I scroll my name in the book and put the pen down. The director is chewing on her lip looking like she is going to be sick. I pull my shades off and look at her quizzically.

"This has never happened before, and I'm afraid we aren't prepared to handle something like this. I think maybe it's a good idea if Brielle stays home a few days until things settle down," she says blushing beet red.

"I think it is fair to say that this will be Ellie's last day here. I will make a check out for the month for any inconvenience, but as you aren't prepared for this type of thing, I think its best her mother and I find some place that is," I retort.

The poor woman looks deflated. She starts to wring her hands and nods her head. "I'm so sorry to hear that. Brielle is loved here. We will be sorry to see her go. I guess we should go get her things," she says with sincere sadness.

I start to feel that I may have been a little harsh and rash in my words. I know putting Ellie in a different daycare now would be best, but I also know Tamara would have wanted to make that decision. I can't seem to stop digging holes today, but this one is about our baby's safety. I will stand on my decision now.

Cynthia leads us to Ellie's class, and we clean out her cubby. The teacher and assistants all fawn over Ellie, wishing her well and saying their goodbyes as news spreads that Ellie will not be returning. Their words to Ellie are heartfelt and sincere, but it does not stop them from ogling me. It is a little uncomfortable to have my daughter's teachers drooling at me.

Once Ellie's things are packed up, I scoop her up in my arms and grab her now overstuffed bag. Cynthia walks us toward the door looking like she is going to faint.

"Excuse me Mr. Monroe, but I am such a big fan and if I don't ask it is going to haunt me. Can I please have your autograph," Cynthia asks as we near the door.

I chuckle. "It's Brad and sure no problem." I am in a better mood now that I have Ellie, and she is calm.

"Brad, okay," she gushes pulling a sticky pad from her back pocket and a sharpie from another. "Thank you so much. I'm so glad you decided to come back home and play. I followed your career in college as well."

I autograph her sticky note and hand it back to her with the pen. "Thanks for the support. Miss. Daly –,"

"Oh please, Cynthia," she interrupts me.

"I would appreciate if you and everyone here would respect my family and our privacy. Please don't go out there sharing anything disclosed to you in confidence and if your staff could do the same, it would be great. Maybe I can get the kids here in for a field trip at the stadium for your cooperation," I offer.

"Oh Brad, you don't have to worry, I will ensure the staff remains professional," Cynthia assures me gaining some composure and pushing her shoulders back.

"Thank you again," I say to her as I slip my shades back on. "You ready baby?" I ask Ellie. She gives me a bright smile and nods her head. "Put your face in my neck Sugar and keep it there until daddy gets you safe in the car, okay?"

"Yes," Ellie says then buries her face into my neck.

My security surrounds us, and we are off, heading straight for my truck as the men shield us with their bodies as best they can. I'd bought Ellie a seat just for my car yesterday. It broke my heart the day she wanted to ride with me, and I wasn't prepared. Something in my gut told me to put her seat in place this morning before I took off.

Once I have her strapped in, I place her bag inside and get in behind the wheel. I sigh as some of the stress lifts. I pull out my phone and text Tam right away. I sit thinking of where to go from here. I don't have a key to Tamara's place, and Ellerie won't be available for a while. He was supposed to pick Ellie up at four and drop her home and unlock the door for me to watch her until Tam gets home.

I haven't asked Tam for a key or anything because I want to respect her space and her need to take things slow. I sigh because there is only one solution. I need a shower and a change of clothes. Tamara is going to be pissed, but what else am I supposed to do.

"Sugar, how would you like to go meet some people important to Daddy?"

"Yay," Ellie squeals.

Well, decision made we're going to meet the family.

Chapter 14

"Mama," I call through the house, as I walk through the front door carrying a groggy Brielle inside. She'd fallen asleep on the ride over.

"In the kitchen Brad," she calls back. I walk into the kitchen to find her hanging halfway out of the pantry. "Is everything okay, you're home early?" She steps out of the pantry and stops in her tracks.

One hand flies to her heart, and the other goes shakily over her mouth as she sucks in a breath of air. Her eyes fill with tears as she just stares at Ellie. I can't stop smiling. I am so proud to finally have my mama meet my little girl.

I sit at one of the breakfast bar stools and place Ellie on my lap. My mother quickly washes and dries her hands on a towel. She walks around to stand before us keeping her eyes on Ellie the whole time. Ellie watches her with curious eyes.

"Ellie, this is your grandma, Grandma Gloria," I say gently.

Ellie's face lights up, and she smiles that beautiful smile up at my mama. Ellie looks back and forth between us then clasps her hands with her own little revelation. "I have another grandma in New York; her name is Nana. She's my mommy's mommy. Are you my daddy's mommy?" Ellie asks with wonder.

"Yes honey, I am," my mama chokes.

"Oh, it's so nice to meet you. My name is Brielle Nicole Hathaway. My birthday is July 14th, I'll be four this year, my favorite colors are blue and purple, I love to read and write, and I know my address, but I'm not supposed to tell that to strangers," Ellie gushes, she blushes then peeks up at me. "But Grandmas are not strangers, right Daddy?"

"Not anymore, Sugar," I croak.

Ellie beams and turns back to my mama holding out her little arms for a hug. "I love hugs," Ellie says coyly.

"Oh honey, I love to give them," my mama says folding Ellie into a tight embrace.

"That's a good one."

I laugh when my mama finally releases her.

"Oh Brad, she is everything you said and more," my mama says with trembling lips. "She has your eyes and your dimples. Oh, I have to call your father. He went to go riding at the ranch. He'll turn back around. I know your brother and sister will want to be here too. I'll call them right away. I'll cook up something special for tonight."

I don't have the heart to tell her no and I know this is just getting me deeper into trouble, but I can't see that smile on her face crushed. She already has the phone in her hand dialing before finishing her thought. I shake my head and chuckle to myself.

"Mama, I need to shower and change, can Ellie sit here. Maybe you can make her a turkey sandwich. She'll tell you how she likes it," I say as she waits for the person on the other end to answer.

"Sure honey…Vernon hold on," my mother says as my father answers on the other end, "go on Brad, us girls will be fine."

I stand, placing Ellie on the stool I'd been sitting on and push her closer to the island. She looks so cute with her legs dangling and a smile on her face. It is hard to believe that just a couple of hours ago she was so upset. Mama is already on to her next call as I exit the room heading upstairs to my room.

Dressed in a fresh pair of jeans and a button down shirt rolled up over my elbows I make my way back downstairs. I am looking through my text messages as I hear the laughter rising toward me from the kitchen. I reply to Tamara and send the message. As I look up, I see the kitchen island is full of my family, including my baby at the center of everyone's attention.

Daddy and mama flank her sides, as my brother stands with his hip propped up against the counter and his legs crossed at the ankles. Ann is leaning on the counter with her elbows, beaming at Ellie until she notices me in the room. Ann pops up and rushes over to give me a tight hug.

"She so beautiful," she sobs in my shoulder. Ann is five nine, so she is not that much shorter than me. "God Brad, I can't believe she is only four. She is amazing, and she absolutely adores you."

"I adore her too," I chuckle. I am trying to hold back my own tears.

I've battled in the beginning with whether or not I should be mad at Tamara for not reaching out to tell me about Ellie. I know it is more my fault than hers. I knew we had unprotected sex, and I still chose to leave without a word.

I had never had sex without a condom before or after Tamara. It wasn't like I made a habit of going around jumping into bed with just anyone. I should have thought of all the repercussions of my actions. I know I owe Tamara way more than what I had given her that night.

Seeing Brielle with my family now shows me how many people my poor choice really hurt. I'd do anything to fix that now. I know I plan to spend the rest of my life making up for the time I lost with Ellie.

"Daddy, guess what," Ellie squeals when she looks over at me. "Papa...he said I can call him Papa since I call Grandpa Byron, Pop-pop. Papa said that I have my own pony, and he's going to teach me how to ride it. Daddy, I always wanted a pony!'"

I groan. My dad gives all the kids their own horse. I wouldn't think Brielle would be any different. I just don't know what Tamara will think of our daughter horseback riding.

"Baby, that's great, but we're going to have to ask your mama if that's okay first, Sugar," I say softly.

"Oh," Ellie says as her little face falls. She looks down at her hands in her lap and furrows her brows. Suddenly her face brightens, and her head snaps up. "She'll be okay with it Daddy."

I laugh. "Oh yeah, what makes you so sure," I ask.

"Mommy used to ride horses when she was a girl," Ellie says proudly.

"How do you know that?"

"I saw pictures, and she has trophies and ribbons. There in her room at Nana and Pop pop's house. Mommy used to be a dancer too Daddy. She has ballet slippers in her old room. I go to dance too, but I have to wait until Uncle Eli finishes with football work to start again. Auntie Stacey used to take me when Uncle Eli couldn't but she is in Europe now modeling. So I have to wait until Mommy finds a new after school sitter who can take me or wait for Uncle Eli to finish winning the Super Bowl."

We all laugh. She sounds so sure Ellerie will win the Super Bowl and being on the same team with him now I hope she is right. Ellie is just full of information. I know Tamara has a nice body and stays in shape, but I didn't know she danced. I also didn't realize she knew anything about horses. I will definitely have to get her out to the ranch. I haven't had a girlfriend that could handle a horse since high school.

"Oh Brad, maybe she can join the girls dance school, and I could take her. Trev's girls go with mine," Ann says excitedly.

"Really," Ellie beams.

"Whoa guys, thanks, Ann, but you guys have got to stop promising her stuff that I'm not sure her mama will be okay with. I'm in enough trouble as it is," I sigh.

"Oh Brad, I'm so sorry. Her excitement is just so infectious," Ann giggles.

"Tell me about it. I already promised to come to her house to swim in the pool," my brother Trevor chuckles.

I throw my head back and groan. I draw a hand down my face and sigh. "Ellie baby, whatever everyone here has promised you today we are going to have to run it all by your mama. Now if she says no to any of it, you can't give her a hard time about it like you did this morning, you hear me," I say gently. "That tantrum you threw this morning can't happen again."

"Okay," Ellie whispers. "I just wanted to wear my pins to show Miss. Cynthia and Mrs. Jenny. They always talk about how pretty Mommy is and how nice her jewelry and clothes are. I just wanted to be pretty like Mommy."

"Sugar, you're just as pretty as your mama with or without those pins," I tell her warmly.

"Really Daddy," she says with a toothy smile.

"Yeah baby, you are."

"Mommy's so pretty Uncle Eli's friend; Mike wanted to marry her," Ellie beams proudly.

I rock back on my heels at her words and Trev lets out a low whistle. "Sounds like you have a little competition," Trev chuckles and raises a brow.

"Shut up," I growl.

My head is spinning. Tamara said she hadn't been with anyone since me. She told me she wasn't dating. I had never thought there was anyone else to worry about. I never thought she would lie.

"I don't think you have anything to worry about," Ann chirps. "I saw the paper and the pictures on the news. She looks like she is completely in love with you."

"Pictures in the news?" my mother bristles.

"You can't tell me you didn't know they were out there," Trev snorts.

"I wasn't thinking. I should have known better; I should have thought about protecting Ellie. I messed up," I mutter.

"Speaking of which, why isn't she in school? Is that why you're in the doghouse, because you kept her home today," Trevor asks.

I sigh, "No, the reporters ambushed Ellie at daycare and Tam had to be in a meeting. I was the only one that could get to Ellie."

"Oh, that's terrible," my mama gasps.

"Ellie, how about you join your Papa to watch some T.V., and we let these old folks talk," my father says to Ellie as he stands. Ellie nods her head happily, and my dad helps her down from her stool.

Once they are out of the room the fun starts. My mama and siblings take turns asking questions about what I plan to do with the new turn of events. I spill to them everything I have no answers to. I am still trying to figure this all out, being with Tam, having a family and not messing up with each decision I make.

Chapter 15

Today has been the longest day of my life. When I walk into my house and kick off my shoes, I just want to see my baby girl and have a glass of wine. It dawns on me when I notice the house is quiet that Brad and Brielle aren't here.

I thought Ellerie would have let them in by now. Brad doesn't have a key to come and go so I am a little freaked out. I fish my phone out of my purse hurriedly.

"Hey Darlin'," Brad drawls. I can hear laughter and talking in the background.

"Brad, where are you? I thought Ellerie would have let you guys in by now. Did something happen," I rush.

"I told him not to come. We were across town when he said he was on the way."

"Bradley, where are you?"

"I'm at my parents' house, well my house for now until I find a place. I needed to shower and change after I picked Ellie up. Then my mama called the rest of the family over and I sort of lost track of time," Brad explains.

"Brad," I groan. "What part of taking things slow don't you get? I don't get it. This is just so out of control. Just bring my daughter home, Bradley."

"Now wait a minute Darlin', Ellie is safe and happy. She's playing with her cousins and getting to know her family. I was hoping you would come here and meet my family too. My mama cooked a big spread, and she would love to have you here," Bradley says, sounding anxious and frustrated all at once.

I am just pissed. I feel like I am just having things thrown at me left and right and I am not getting a say in any of it. Things haven't been this out of control in my life in a really long time.

"You know this isn't fair to me. I just asked you to do one thing, and now I'm the bad person if I say no. I'm so tired Brad. I didn't need this today. I've had the day from hell, and this is not what I need. I'm not prepared to meet your family, but does that matter to you, no, because *you*... as always enter my life and turn it upside down and leave me to pick up the pieces."

Brad sighs heavily into the phone and is quite for a moment. "I'm sorry Tam. We'll be there in an hour," he finally says.

I pinch the bridge of my nose and squeeze my eyes shut. "No Brad, text me the address. I'll come to you," I say as calmly as I can.

"Are you sure?"

"Yes Brad, it's best this way."

~B~

I curse and bang my head against the wall under the stairs once I hang up the phone and text Tam my parents' address. That conversation went worse than I thought. Tamara is right. I could have handled this better. I am being unfair to her.

She sounded so pissed off at me. It's just that watching Ellie with my family has been so great. When Ann and Trevor's kids got here, Ellie was so excited to meet them all. They took right to her.

She's been locked on Jessica's hip, my oldest niece, ever since they said hi to each other. Each time they enter the kitchen Ellie is dangling from Jess's side. Ellie looks so happy. You'd think she grew up with all the rest of the kids. I just want Tam to be a part of this. I didn't think about how tired and stressed she'd be.

I sigh and shove off the wall to head back into the kitchen with the adults. Ann's husband, Tom, and Trev's wife, Donna, have both arrived with the kids. Ann has three kids, and Trev has four. Everyone looks up when I reenter the room. I had been so happy when I saw it was Tam calling. Now I look like someone kicked my dog.

"Everything okay," my mama asks with concern.

"Yeah, Tam just had a long day, and I should have considered that," I huff.

"Oh honey, I can pack a few plates for y'all and you could take her something to eat," Mama offers already moving to get supplies to do so.

"No, she's on her way already."

"Well, now that she's snagged a pro football star, she won't have to work so hard," Donna says smugly.

"Not everyone is out for a paid day to flit around doing what they please," Ann growls.

Trevor snorts and glares at his wife. I do my best to ignore her because I am not sure I'll be able to reign in my temper right now. My mama is trying not to glare and failing horribly, which is out of character for Gloria Monroe. Donna knows how to get under everyone's skin.

"I'm just saying, what do you know about this woman? Who's her family? Are you sure that little girl is yours?" Donna snarls.

"I don't see how any of that is your business," Trevor snaps, "although, I sure should have asked more of those questions before getting involved with you."

"Oh please Trevor," Donna snorts and rolls her eyes. "I mean she's black right? I think if you were going to experiment with groupies you would have been more careful. Now you have a little half breed. No telling what this mistake could cost you."

I feel myself growl all the way from my toes and just barely realized my brother is doing the same. We are like two overgrown bears in the middle of my mama's kitchen. Ann's face is bright red, and she is clenching her fists, but it is my mama that speaks first.

"Donna, I have not raised my children that way. Brielle is no different from any of my other grandchildren no matter who her mother is. Tamara has done an amazing job with Ellie, and she has made my son happier than I have seen him in a very long time. I think it best if you keep your opinions to yourself, Donna. I don't want them breathed in my home," my mama's chest is practically heaving when she is done.

"My daughter is no mistake," I bite out. "Tam is not some money hungry groupie; she's the woman I plan to marry and have more children with."

"Oh," Donna gasps as her head snaps back like she's been slapped. "I hope she's worth it." She murmurs with a sour face.

"I think I need a beer, come on bro," Trevor grunts.

"I think I'll join you guys," Ann's husband says clearing his throat. "Try to behave." It is a whisper meant for Ann before we all head for the garage.

Mama and daddy have kept an old sofa out in the garage for us since we were teens. I guess the tradition followed from the ranch. Trev pulls three beers from the cooler and flops down between Tom and me.

"I don't know what to do anymore. She's the mother of my kids, but that's about it, I don't love her. Hell, I don't think she even cares about any of us. I don't even know who she is. You do know none of us feel that way? The things she said in there. We haven't even met the girl yet. But from what you tell us she sounds a hell of a lot better than what I tied myself to," Trevor sighs heavily and downs his whole beer.

"Trev, we come from the same mama and daddy. I know you wouldn't think half of the things Donna says out loud. She has never known how to keep her trap shut. I wouldn't have let it get to me in the first place if I wasn't already on edge," I reassure him.

"Donna hates herself, buddy; it has nothing to do with you or the kids. You're doing a great job with the kids, and you know Ann and I are always ready to help, anytime," Tom says sympathetically.

"Something has to change soon. I can't keep doing this. I can't keep pretending that she's not spending way too much or that it isn't a big deal when she is supposed to be taking care of the kids, and I get called away from a job to cover for her. You haven't been home Brad. You haven't seen how bad she can really be. She actually mouthed off to daddy for not giving the ranch or the CEO position of Monroe Oil over to me."

"Wow Trev, I knew things were tense. TAB Construction has been a great success. We all invested a lot into it, and you've delivered big time. Daddy knows your heart is in building. We've known for years, he was going to hand things over to Cousin Cliff," I rumble out loud.

"Yeah, well that greedy bitch thinks all the money comes from daddy, the ranch, and the oil." Trevor sighs. "I don't know, after she got pregnant with Jess, I had this gut feeling I shouldn't let on that I planned to build TAB. That's why I've had Tom as my front man all this time. Keeping her thinking, I work for my best friend and brother in law has been for the best.

"She doesn't know about the books and things like that, she'd just spend it all. To this day, she still doesn't know TAB stands for Trevor, Ann, and Brad. Once daddy put everything in place for me to get started and you guys fronted me the money mom helped with the books when I needed it.

"Now Ann makes sure you guys get your checks, and the guys get paid. If Donna really knew how much money was really circulating around here, she'd drain every dime. Only thing that keeps her off sites is that she doesn't want to get dirty. Otherwise, she may have figured it out by now." Trevor chuckles and shakes his head getting up to get another beer.

I just let my brother vent. Through talking to Ann, I already knew some of this. Trevor and I are close, but Ann and I are a lot closer for several reasons. Trevor, being ten years older, never leans on us as much as we lean on him. He started his construction company when Ann and I graduated high school. Since Ann and I were finally old enough to touch our funds, the whole family chipped in to help out.

Jess was six at the time. Things weren't great with Donna then, but Trev was in love with Jess, and Toby, and Paige were soon to follow. To be honest, I think Donna got pregnant with the twins because Trevor was talking about taking Jessica and leaving. Same thing when they had Jonathan. Trevor met Donna when he was in college. Mama never was too keen on her, but then she got pregnant, and the rest is history.

"Things will work themselves out," Tom sighs.

"Yeah, like they worked out with you marrying our sister?" Trev snorts.

"Buddy, it's been nine years now, and you know how much I love Ann," Tom shakes his head and takes a sip of his beer.

"Bro, she's my baby sister and you are my best friend, who happens to be ten years older than she is. I'm going to give you shit 'til we're old and grey," Trev says smugly.

I'm happy they can joke about this now because it was pretty ugly when everyone figured out that Tom and Ann were seeing each other. I remember it being a little weird at first to see the two of them together, but Tom really does love my sister. The ten year age difference has never been a problem for the two of them. Tom says Ann keeps him young.

"Well, I think I'd rather give Brad here a little shit. I heard that remark about getting married back there. So this is finally the one?" Tom asks with a warm smile. He has always been like another older brother to me.

"I was going to get around to that. I was thinking the same thing. Are you sure you want to go and get married? All of

these women will drive you crazy. At least, when you are just
dating you can run," Trevor snorts then laughs.

"I don't know what made me say that in there, but I guess
it came from the heart. Yeah, I want to marry Tam. I know
we have a lot to work out and learn about each other, but I've
wanted to be with her for so long. She just feels like home."

"Well, little brother, you have my blessing. I can only hope
to find that someday," Trevor presses his lips and glares at
the door that leads back to his wife.

We move on to talking about football and drinking more
beer. After an hour, I start watching my phone every minute
to see if I missed Tam's call or something. She should have
been here by now. I am starting to get worried. Everything
flashes through my mind from her being run off the road to
her being lost out there somewhere.

I know she has been in Texas for five years, but these
roads out here can be tricky. As the second-hour approaches,
I am ready to come out of my skin. I have gone in to check
on Ellie and make sure Tamara didn't ring the front doorbell,
and I missed it or something. Being in the garage, we should
be the first to hear her drive up, so I am not surprised not to
see her in the house.

"Brad, have you tried to call Tamara. It's getting late, and dinner is just about ready," Mama asks as she pulls some biscuits from the oven.

"I was trying to give her time. She's driving you know?"

Just as my mother is about to protest my phone starts to ring. I quickly pull the phone from my pocket. Gesturing to my mama that it is Tamara and I am going to take it.

"Everything okay, Sweetheart," I say into the phone. "Where are you?"

"I'm out front," she replies on a huff. "Can you come out?"

"Yeah, be right out."

I rush out the side door to the garage and out the little door attached. I get halfway to the car when I stop in my tracks. Tamara is standing with the passenger side door open, but that's not what stops me.

I've never seen Tamara looking like this. She'd completely changed from what she was wearing when I saw her this morning. Even her hair is different. I am used to her wearing it up or it tumbling down her back in long curls or waves. She has straightened it making it almost hit the center of her back,

and her bangs are sweeping across her face and feathered out.
I knew her hair was pretty long, but it looks amazing this way
as it curls under at the tips and bounces and blows around
her in the light breeze.

It doesn't just stop with the hair. Her lips are tinted a
flattering shade of pink almost plum. There is a plum-colored
scarf tied around her neck. The black silk button down blouse
she is wearing is fitted, and the top buttons are left open
revealing a plum tank top. Her light blue jeans are like a
second skin and just to show me she is meant for me she has
on a pair of calf high, heeled black cowgirl boots.

I draw a hand down my jaw and release the breath I hadn't
realized I was holding. Tamara looks up at me through her
lashes and smirks. She knows she's killing me, doesn't she? I
close the distance between us placing my hands on her hips
hoping she isn't still too pissed to let me touch her.

"You take my breath away," I bend to murmur against her
lips. I am so relieved when she returns the kiss. I groan into
her open mouth. I try to deepen the kiss tipping her head
back, but she pulls away giggling up at me.

"Brad," she breathes and peeks nervously around me at the house. "I want to see Bri. Can you carry this box in for me?"

"Sure," I steal one more kiss before side stepping her, reaching in the truck for the box on the seat. I peek inside, then turn to look at her. "What is all this?"

"My mother taught me you never show up to dinner at someone's home empty-handed," she shrugs with a little smile.

I think she is really nervous. I have never seen her nervous. Tam is so confident all the time. I tuck the box under my arm and grab her purse off the seat, turning to hand it to her. Once she takes her purse, I close the door to the truck and wrap my free arm around her, kissing the top of her head.

"Relax Darlin', they're going to love you," I reassure her.

"Um-hm, *sure*," she murmurs under her breath. Tamara looks up at me and shakes her head as she quickly reaches to wipe her lip gloss from my lips.

Before we can make it all the way to the front door it flies open and my mama and daddy, stand beaming at us. Brielle squeezes between the two of them and shoots into Tamara's arms. I can feel some of the tension leave Tamara's body but not all of it.

"Mommy," Ellie squeals.

"Hey baby, I missed you today. How's my baby?"

"Mommy, I had so much fun today. I met Grandma Gloria and Papa and Jess, Auntie Ann, Uncle Trev, Uncle Tom, Jonathan, Paige, Toby, Amy, George, and Melissa. Oh, and Mrs. Donna. Papa gave me a pony and said he's going to teach me to ride it. Can I learn, Mommy, *please*," Ellie rambles, and I groan.

"Sugar, I thought we talked about that," I sigh.

"You said we had to ask Mommy," Ellie murmurs.

Tamara giggles. "Brielle have you been driving your father crazy all day."

"No," Ellie replies with a little frown.

"Well, me and your daddy will talk about your pony and your lessons. From what I remember your Daddy said your Papa is great with horses," Tam beams at Ellie.

Tam is taking the pony situation a lot better than I thought she would. I guess she is just really happy to see Brielle safe and happy. Ellie hugs her tightly around the neck and places her head on her shoulder.

"Come on you two," I beam pushing Tam forward into the house.

Mama and daddy back up to give us some room to enter the house. Everyone else is packed into the foyer behind them. I feel my chest swell with pride as I walk in the door with my girls.

"Mama, Daddy, this is Tamara. Tamara this is my mama, Gloria Monroe and my daddy, Vernon Monroe," I start the introductions.

"Hello, it's so nice to meet you," Tamara says nervously, as she plays with her fingers.

"Honey, you are just the cutest thing ever. I see why my son is so taken with you," my mama coos as she engulfs Tam in a big hug.

"Thank you, Mrs. Monroe," Tam smiles.

"Oh, you stop that. Call me Gloria. I'm so happy to finally get to meet you and Ellie. I won't dare have you getting all formal on me. We're all family here."

"It's so good to meet you, Tamara. Sorry about the pony Darlin'," my father blushes as he rubs the back of his neck. "I give one to all the grands. I already have hers picked out for her, but her lessons are up to you. She can go to the ranch and just pet her pony any time."

"It's fine Mr. Monroe. I loved horseback riding when I was a little girl. Brielle is a lucky little girl to get her very own pony," Tam says with a big smile.

"Vernon, call me Vernon or you can call me Papa like Ellie here."

"Okay," Tam laughs.

"So does that mean I can talk you into going riding with me," I lean into Tam's ear to whisper.

"Maybe," she looks up at me and replies. Tamara reaches into the box I am holding and pulls out one gift basket and two envelopes. "Vernon, Gloria, thank you for having me in your home. This isn't much; I wish I had better notice." Tamara looks over at me and narrows her eyes.

"Oh honey, you didn't have to do this," my mother coos. "Thank you so much."

"Okay, Mama, let the rest of us get a turn," Ann teases, bouncing over to Tamara and pulling her into a hug. "I'm Ann, Bradley's twin sister."

"Oh my God, you're a twin," Tamara says in shock looking back and forth between Ann and me.

"Runs in the family, hon," Ann laughs waving over her family. "These are my twins, George, and Melissa, my baby Amy and my husband, Tom."

"It's so nice to meet you all," Tamara says giving a nervous smile and turning to the box again. "Um, I have something for the kids too. I was hoping I got this right. Brad said he had four nieces and three nephews."

Tamara hands George a blue envelope that looks like it holds a card. She then turns to the girls handing them both a large envelope in pink for each of them. The kids beam at her as they each accept their gifts, murmuring and exclaiming, 'thanks, ma'am' and 'thank you, Miss. Tamara.'

"You're all very welcome, and you can call me Tam."
Reaching back in the box, she pulls out a large gift bag and
two more envelopes handing them to Ann and Tom.

"Oh Tam, you really shouldn't have," Ann says.

"Well, let me get a good look first and then we'll say
whether or not she shouldn't have," Tom teases with a warm
smile for Tam.

"Ha, I may not have had much time or warning but I
think I did okay," Tam laughs at Tom.

"Well, I like you without the gifts already," Ann beams.

"Next," Trev booms and nudges Ann aside. I chuckle and
shake my head at my siblings.

"This is my older brother Trevor and his family. Jessica is
the oldest –," I start.

"Jess is my new best friend," Ellie breaks in beaming at
her cousin. Jess laughs and strokes Ellie's hair.

"It is great to meet you, Jess," Tamara laughs reaching in
the box for a pink envelope and whispering in Ellie's ear
before turning to the box and pulling out the last gift bag
handing it to Trev. "Nice to meet you as well, Trevor."

"Great to put a face to the name, this is my wife Donna, my twins, Toby and Paige, and my youngest, Jonathan," Trevor finishes the introductions, while I took the last of the envelopes from the box and help Tam place one in everyone's hand. "What do you say, kids?"

"Thanks, Tam," the kids chime in unison.

"You're all very welcome," Tamara beams.

I had two extra envelopes still in my hands. I look at Tam and raise a brow at her. She smiles plucking the pink envelope from my hand. "You didn't think I'd leave you out did you?"

I nuzzle her neck. "You're what I really want right now," I whisper in her ear. "You're so adorable all nervous."

"Wow, Uncle Brad she gave us tickets to see the Rangers, Astros, Rockets, Spurs, Cowboys and Texans. Dude, you never did anything this cool," Toby croons.

"So you're going to sell me out that easy," I grumble.

"Alright, now we can all open our gifts later. Dinner is getting cold," Mama announces, rounding up the crew.

She is already too late. Everyone is squealing in appreciation as they open gifts to either sporting events or a spa retreat. Tam nailed it. She found something to make everyone happy and give us time to be a family together. She already fits in perfectly.

Chapter 16

Dinner went better than I could have ever have dreamed. My family took Tam in as if she has been here a million times over the years. Well, everyone except Donna, who glared at Tamara throughout dinner. She made a few snide remarks that had my brother hissing in her ear.

For the most part, Tam ignored her, as did everyone else. After my mama's peach cobbler and some homemade ice cream, we all retired to the living room. Tam went to sit beside me, but I quickly pulled her into my lap, nuzzling her neck.

"My family loves you," I murmur against her skin. "I can tell my mama really likes you."

"I like her too," Tam chuckles back, "she doesn't hold anything back does she?"

"Not at all," I throw my head back and laugh.

"I think I better get Bri ready to go. I have a busy day tomorrow," Tam informs me.

"I can watch Ellie tomorrow," I offer.

"I was actually going to take the day off. I have a lot that I have been putting off concerning Bri. I might as well get it all taken care of," Tam shrugs. "Besides, you have practice tomorrow."

Before I can reply, Donna is opening her trap. "I guess snapping up Bradley Monroe is working out well for you. You'll never have to work again," Donna sneers.

"Excuse me," Tamara's head snaps around to glare at Donna.

"What is it that you said you do again?" Donna says, ignoring Tam's words.

"I didn't say," Tam hisses. "But trust me. I have no intentions of living off of Brad and his money, so you have no worries there."

"Oh, honey, please. You saw a payday and took it right away. Can you really say for sure that that little girl is Brad's," Donna snarls.

"Donna," my mother growls.

"No, please let me," Tam answers. "It seems that she has had this on her chest all night so let me put her in her place. My family alone nets more than Bradley's new contract. My trust fund would make you blush, and then there is the fact that I am one of the top attorneys in my firm and in line for partnership. Neither my daughter nor I need a dime from Brad, never have and never will.

"As far as Brad being Brielle's father, I don't know what kind of woman you are sweetie, but I know who the father of my daughter is without question," Tam turns to me with her chest heaving. "Brad I have to find my daughter a new school in the morning, so I better go."

"Baby, we will find *our* daughter a new school in the morning," I say a little harsher than I mean to. I am not pissed at Tam. I am livid with Donna.

"We are going to be on our way," Ann says sadly, as she glares at Donna. "Tam, Brad the kids have a half day tomorrow it would be no trouble at all if you wanted to let

Ellie sleep over at my place. Ellie could spend the morning with me. It would give you and Brad time to take care of things."

"Thanks, Ann, but you don't have to," Tam smiles at my sister's warm offer.

"It would be no trouble at all," Ann reassures her.

Tam looks at me and chews on her bottom lip. I wrap my arms around her waist, pulling her against my chest. "It would help us to get more done. I know you have wanted a sitter for after school, we can look into that."

Tam sighs and rubs her temples.

"Come on Tamara, you are not alone in this. Let us help," my dad encourages with a broad smile.

"Okay, I guess it couldn't hurt, but are you sure it will be okay?" Tam relents.

"Sure hon, it will be fine. The kids love her, and I will enjoy some company around the house tomorrow," Ann replies with a wide smile.

"Thanks, Ann," I say as I see Tam mentally caving.

"I always keep an extra set of clothes in the car. Let me get them and see if Bri is okay with the idea," Tam says totally ignoring the presence of a now huffy Donna.

As soon as Tam steps out of hearing distance I whirl around on Donna. "Don't you ever disrespect my family again, not my woman, not my daughter or any of my future children. I don't care who you are married to," I growl.

"I think it is time for you to leave my home, Donna," my father says calmly. "It would do you some good not to come back here until you learn some manners."

"Really," Donna gasps.

"Really," Trevor snaps. "Mama, Dad, I apologize for my wife."

"Son, we know exactly who we raised. This is not on you," Mama says gently.

"I'll round up the kids," Ann says before giving me a hug and exiting the room.

Donna storms out without thought of her children or her husband. Realizing Donna is heading in the same direction Tam has gone I rush out to follow only to find Tam is already helping Ann get the children together to make their way home.

Ellie looks up at me through sleepy eyes with a huge smile on her tired little face. "Daddy, guess what? I get to sleep over at Aunt Ann and Uncle Tom's house," Ellie sings tiredly.

I reach to take her from Tam's arms to carry her out to Ann's car. "That's good baby girl. I want you to be good for your aunt and uncle and have fun, okay," I kiss my baby girl's forehead and beam with pride to have such an adorable and smart little girl.

"I will Daddy," Ellie says with a sage nod of her head.

I can tell Tam is exhausted by the time we get Ellie in the car with my sister and her kids. We each climb in our trucks and start for her place. I know she is tired when she watches me toss my bags in my truck and only shakes her head and laughs in protest, not at all the fight I thought we would have over me sleeping over tonight.

I drive close behind her on the way to her place to insure she is okay. That is why I become alarmed when we turn into her block, and her car comes to a halt. I pull around her SUV to her driver's side to see what is going on, and that is when I see the reporters and cameras surrounding the front of her home.

I pinch the bridge of my nose as all the blood drains from my face. I'm just not going to catch a break, am I? Before I can signal for Tam to roll her window down, she floors it and rushes through the crowd pulling into the garage door. I hadn't noticed it open.

I quickly follow her inside. The door is already closing by the time I make it inside, and cameras are flashing behind us. Once the door fully closes, Tam is out the car slamming the door behind her so hard I am surprised the window didn't crack.

She rushes into the house closing the side door loudly as well. I slowly make my way into the house happy she hasn't locked me out. I follow the sound of her boots stomping and more doors slamming. I am in no rush for the fight that is ahead of me.

I make my way upstairs to the closed bedroom door. With a deep sigh, I open the door and sag in relief to hear the shower going and see the bathroom door closed. This I could do, if I can distract Tam, I can buy myself some time. I start to strip out of my own clothes.

I walk to the bathroom door and nod to myself when I turn the knob, and it too is unlocked. I step into the bathroom and lose my thoughts at the sight of the woman I love standing beneath the water with her head against the tiles. However, my thoughts come crashing back down when I realize that her shoulders are shaking as the water rolls down her spine.

The sight is killing me. I never want to see this woman in pain. Just the thought itself has my feet moving toward her. I step into the shower and wrap my arms around her waist. I nuzzle her neck, but Tam stiffens in my arms. I curse in my thoughts and move to turn her to face me. I reach up and wipe the tears from her cheeks. It is literally tearing me up to see this strong woman reduced to tears.

"Talk to me baby," I plead.

"I worked so hard to put my life together after meeting you. The one time I do something so out of my character, it bites me in the biggest way ever," Tam sobs. "I finally have things in my life in order, and here you are again. I wanted to take this slow, and now I have reporters camping out outside my daughter's daycare and my home. I didn't ask for this I don't want this for Brielle and me."

"Now wait a minute there," I seethe. "Brielle is our daughter. I was just as upset and worried about her as you. I care about you Tam, and it is killing me to see you like this. I had no intention to come and disturb your life, but I have a right to be a part of Brielle's life, and I want to be a part of yours if you will let me. But Tam, I am who I am, and you know all about my career, you deal with your clients all the time. You had to know that it was possible that dating me would change some things in your life."

"I don't want this," Tam snaps. "I don't want to be in the spotlight, I don't want your family thinking I want you for your money, I don't want to be in love with you. I didn't ask for any of this."

I lock eyes with her as her word sink in. There are a few words that I am hearing loud and clear above all the rest. I cup her face in the palms of my hands, crushing her plump lips with mine. I kiss her deeply and feel her moan vibrate through my chest as I taste her salty tears on my tongue.

"Say it for me Darlin'," I groan against her lips.

Tam pulls back with a confused look on her face. "Say what?"

"Tell me you love me," I smile down at her.

She frowns and slaps a hand against my wet chest. "Is that all you heard me say?" She snaps with no real bite.

"It was the most important thing that you said. Now say it for me, Baby," I reply as I back her up against the shower wall.

She pinned her hair up, this time, so I figure I am in the clear this time around. Even if I am not, I am so turned on by her words that I can't think pass what I want to hear.

"Brad, I love you but….," I cut off the rest of her words with a hard kiss to her lips.

I grab two hands full of her warm round backside and lift her until her legs wrap around my waist. I thought it would take a lot more and a lot longer for Tam to admit that she loves me. But to hear her say it now seals my mind on the fact that I will do anything and everything to make this woman happy and keep her in my life 'til the day I breathe no more.

"Tamara," I groan her name. "I love you, baby. I'm going to fix all of this, I promise."

I drop to my knees holding her up against the shower wall. Hanging her legs over my shoulders, I bury my face between her thighs, pulling her waist to me. Her hips start to rock against my face, and I hum in satisfaction. I'll have to wait until the morning to fix everything else but for right now I can make it all about her.

I love her taste on my tongue. Tamara has the sweetest nectar I have ever tasted. I could spend hours down here. I swear I wish I bottled this shit five years ago to hold me over.

"Brad," Tam moans as her fingers lock in my now damp hair. I flatten the tip of my tongue against her clit then wiggle it before flicking it hard. "Ah, Brad, oh yes, yes, please."

I look up at her face as I devour her core. I have never seen anything as beautiful as my woman falling apart for me. Her lips are parted, her face is twisted in passionate pleasure, and her eyes are staring back at me in awe.

I hold her in place as her body quivers, and she slowly comes down from her own personal bliss. She cups my jaw pulling me up to her. I release her legs and steady her with my hands on her waist. I kiss my way up her body until I get to her lips. Tam groans the moment she tastes herself on my lips and tongue.

I lift her in my arms, and she wraps her legs around my waist. I want her now, but I know this is not the time to add to the drama we have going on. So I turn the water off and carry her back into the bedroom.

"Sex doesn't fix this," Tamara murmurs into my neck.

"No, but you need me as much as I need you," I reply.

"Yeah, I do," she simply says before giving herself to me completely. I suit up quickly to give us both what we need.

She is right, sex won't fix this, but I need her in my soul. I have never wanted or loved a woman the way I love her. My cock is so hard, and I haven't even gotten inside her. I feel this ache in my bones to be buried inside her until we cannot be told apart from each other. As a primal need takes over me, I flip her onto her hands and knees.

Tam gets in position willingly wiggling her plump ass at me. I always try to remember how much bigger than her I am, not wanting to hurt her. But right now I feel like a crazed man. This woman that I walked away from because I thought she couldn't love me, wouldn't see me as a man and not a color, is in my arms and she is in love with me. I love her so damn much.

In this moment, all the bullshit goes out the window. I was young and stupid. If I think about it now, she never said she didn't want me. She said she had never been attracted to a white man before. It was clear that night that I was the exception and knowing what I know now. That Tam hasn't been with another man since me, that she is just plain picky about who she lies with, I feel like a fool for being in my feelings back then. I robbed us of something good.

Never again! I thrust into her hot tight sex, and we both cry out. My nostrils flare, and I tighten my grip on her hips. I am blinded by passion as I piston into her body. My strokes are hard and deep, the sensation of my balls ramming against her sex is sending tingles up my spine.

I reach for her clit pinching and rubbing it through her legs. I know how sensitive her nub is, and I want her to come for me at least twice more before I find my own release. Although, as my eyes drop to her ass I don't know if I can hold out that long, I have never seen a more enticing sight.

I reach for a hand full of hair with my other hand and tug her head back. I lick the sweat from her neck, and I feel her body shiver and her sex tighten around me. "Fuck," I hiss. I put my lips to her ear and whisper. "I love you, and I love when you come all over my cock. I'm never letting you go, Tam. We will work our shit out because I can't live without you."

Her response is the shout of my name as she shatters around me. I bite back my own release and pull out before I lose it. I flip her onto her back and move down her body to devour her sweet pussy once again. I curl my arms around her thighs, locking her into place. In no time, I have her screaming the walls down.

Her hold on my hair is so tight I think she is about to tear it out, but I won't stop, not until I feel her come on my tongue. It doesn't take long for her to start gushing like a geyser. Tamara squirts all over my face. At first, I am shocked. I didn't know she was a squirter, but now that I know I plan to wring it out of her anytime I can.

Satisfied that I have licked up every drop I crawl up her body as she purrs in sated bliss. I lift her legs onto my thighs as I hover over her and slowly lower myself until I am sliding into her nice and easy. I still can't believe how hard I am right now.

I slide my arms beneath her back and cup her shoulders. With one smooth lift, I bring her up from the mattress and cradle her in my arms as I start to rock into her faster as our slick chests press together. Her head leans into the crook of my neck, and I feel her warm mouth suck at the flesh there.

I groan and slide one hand down the center of her back. I go on pure instincts when I slide a hand down her back and slip a digit between her ass cheeks and into her forbidden hole. Instead, of the Tam freak out, I expect she locks her arms around my back, and she bites into my shoulder.

"Shit," I growl thrusting up hard and shoving my other hand in her hair pulling her head back.

"Brad," she moans. It is deep and throaty and such a turn on. "Baby, that feels so good."

"Yeah Baby, you like that?" I grunt as I push my finger in and out.

She gasps and starts to rock and grind her wet pussy into me. "Yes, yes, yes," she cries. "I'm coming."

"Come for me Darlin', give it to your man," I growl. I know I'm going over with her, there is no stopping it this time.

"Bradley," her scream pierces the room.

"Tamara," I bellow back.

She is trembling in my arms, and I can feel our hearts beating as one as they settle. If I didn't know it before, I know it now. Tamara is the only one for me. She is my woman, and I love her with everything I am. I'll make all this right.

Chapter 17

I spent the majority of last night making love to my woman. As tired as Tam was she reached for me just as often as I reached for her throughout the night. Our lovemaking was full of passion and everything we hadn't said out loud to one and other. When we finally did fall asleep Tam told me, she loved me once more before kissing my chest and falling into a deep sleep.

I fell asleep a very happy man, although I woke up confused. I expected to wake up with Tam in my arms. The room is quiet, so I know she is not in the bathroom. I push up off the mattress and plant my bare feet on the floor. I run my hands through my hair to push it out of my face and look over at the clock next to the bed.

It is already eleven in the morning. I hadn't meant to sleep so late. Tamara and I have a lot to do today. I left my bags downstairs, so I go into the bathroom and grab a towel to wrap around my waist. I splash some water on my face and rinse out my mouth before going in search for Tam.

When I get downstairs, I find coffee already brewed. I know Tam has done this just for me, which makes me smile. I make a note to come back for a cup after I find her. I walk toward her home office and hear her voice behind the half closed door.

I push it open and lean against the door frame. Tam is sitting in front of her laptop while on her phone. When she notices me in the room, she looks up at me with a smile, holding up a finger for me to wait.

"Yes, two will be fine. Thank you so much for seeing me today," Tam says to whoever is on the other end of the call.

"What are you up to," I ask with a smirk on my lips as I watch her eyes roam greedily over my towel clad body.

"I booked visits with three of the schools on the top of my list, and I lined up a few interviews for nanny's later this afternoon.

I sigh and lift a brow at her. "Darlin', I thought we were going to do this together?"

"You were sleeping so peacefully, and I know you don't get to sleep in like that, so I just started making some calls. But if you want to join me for the first daycare interview you better get moving. The first one is at noon," Tam says as she closes her laptop and walks around the desk.

I take in the fact that she is already showered, but she is only wearing a robe, thigh highs, and heels. At least, that is all that I can see at the moment. I groan and reach for her waist, pulling her into my arms.

"Oh no Brad, we do not have time," Tam starts to giggle as I place soft kisses down the side of her neck. "Babe."

"You are so beautiful, and you smell great. I don't think I've had enough of you yet," I growl against her ear.

"Remember Ellie. I'll let you have your way with me when she has a new sitter and a new day care," Tam purrs back.

"I'll hold you to that, Sweetheart. Trust me," I say with a smile and peck her on the lips before letting her go.

~B~

After last night, you would think I would be content, but I just barely fought Brad off this morning. We are just making our first appointment because he spent twenty minutes whispering words of love in my ear as I dressed in front of the mirror. By the time I slipped into my black skirt and blue silk blouse, we were rushing to get out of the house.

My mouth is still watering at the sight of Brad in his charcoal grey suit and crisp blue dress shirt. The grey tie is just icing on an already handsome cake. I can't blame the director standing before us for drooling. She is trying her best to be professional, but even so she has looked Brad over more than once.

Brad, for the most part, has paid her no mind other than to ask her questions about our daughter's safety and education. His hand has remained possessively on my lower back as we move through the grounds of the day care. This place comes highly recommended, and it would be great to get Brielle in here.

"Do you have any more questions for me?" The director, Regan asks as we come to the end of the tour.

"I think I have seen enough," Brad responds before I can.

"Well, we can step into my office and discuss enrollment," Regan says to us both, but she looks as if she is having fantasies of just her and Brad stepping into her office.

"If you don't mind, I would like to see the other schools we have appointments with before we make a decision," Brad says firmly before turning to me. "Is that okay, Darlin'?"

"Yes, I was thinking the same thing."

Regan doesn't look too pleased, but she covers it quickly and leads us out. "It was a pleasure to meet you both. I look forward to meeting your little girl and having the opportunity to provide her with the best care," Regan says with a wide smile, stretching her hand out toward Brad.

"Thank you again, we will talk to you soon, either way, we decide," Brad says giving her a firm shake.

"Thank you," I repeat to make sure Regan remembers I am here with Brad.

Our next two appointments go pretty much the same. I was sure things would be different at the last daycare when I saw the male director, but he was just as taken with Brad. At least with him, he was just a huge fan. I feel drained as I sit in the passenger seat of Brad's truck.

We are heading back home to set up for the interviews with the sitters. My mind is all over the place, and I suddenly feel so overwhelmed. I am staring out of the window lost in thought when Brad's voice breaks through.

"Are you thinking about the daycares? I really liked the second one. I think Ellie would too," he muses.

"I actually liked that one too. But that is not what I was thinking about," I press my lips and rub my temples.

"Talk to me Tam. If we want this to work you have to be willing to talk to me," Brad peeks over at me quickly before looking back at the road. Concern laces his words and knits his brow.

I think about where to start. There is so much on my mind. I have so much I need to think about. It feels like my whole life is changing so quickly.

"Where do I begin? You know I used to want to make partner. It was all I dreamed about and worked toward. But I don't know what I want anymore," I relinquish.

"Well, what has changed? I thought you loved your job," Brad looks over at me again.

"You know I really don't know. I had a weird conversation with my boss, and it got me to thinking about what is more important to me," I shrug.

Brad lifts a brow. "What was so weird about it?" He asks.

I bite my lip not sure I want to tell him everything that was said. I am still processing it all. I huff in exasperation and decide to bare all. "He was concerned about us. Well about our relationship and how it will affect my career," I frown at my own words.

"I don't see how that could be his concern," Brad says angrily. "And I don't see how our relationship has any bearing on your career."

I run my hand through his hair and turn to look at him. "But see that's the thing. The way Cyrus put it made me think of how much our relationship can affect a lot of things. He wasn't being negative if that is what you're thinking. He was being …. I don't know, proactive. He wants to help me; he and my father are close friends. I think that is why his words are weighing so heavily," I shake my head.

"Okay, so talk to me. What are you thinking? I mean what do his words have to do with you thinking about not wanting to be partner?"

I pause to see how to state my next words because they are very revealing. "I never thought I would want to change my life for a man, but if I can't have both, I'm not so sure my job would come first anymore," I say with a blush.

Brad ignores the paparazzi and pulls into my garage. He cuts the car off and turns toward me with the brightest grin I have ever seen. "Although I am so happy to hear that I have moved up on your priority list, I would never ask you to choose. I'm your man, so I will make any sacrifices in this relationship. However, Darlin', I believe that we can take on anything as long as we do it together. I know it is not going to be easy to be in a relationship with me.

"I'll be gone a lot for games; there will always be some story about my life that they want to know about or that they have made up. I am green on all this being a father stuff, and I am learning to understand you and how to be a part of your life. We have a lot on our plates, but I think we can make this work if we do it as a family.

"I want this Tam. I want you. I never want to be apart from my family again. You and Ellie are my everything. I will do whatever I have to, to make this work," Bradley says that last part with such conviction I want to believe that we will make it through all of this, but my stomach and the knots in it are telling me it is not going to be that easy.

Just look, they are still camped out in front of my home with cameras. I know I can't live like this. I have a daughter to think about.

"Tam, baby, I see the wheels turning. I've been looking for a place, and I was thinking that it would be better if you and Ellie move with me when I find one. It will be more secure and I just really want you with me," Brad says almost pleadingly.

"This is all so much so fast. I need time to think," I place my head in my hands.

"You have until I find a place, which is now priority so that I can make my girls safe again," Brad says firmly before turning and stepping out of the truck.

I am left a little stunned. This wouldn't be the first time Brad just decided to lay the law down. While, at times, it can be a turn on, right now it is just serving to piss me off.

I glare at Brad as he rounds the truck to open my door. I am still glaring at him when he opens my door and stands waiting for me to get out. He ducks his head into the truck and pecks my lips.

"I love you and my daughter. I'm going to make this work Tam. I will fix it all, which means I need you safe and by my side," he says against my lips.

My shoulders sag. I don't want to fight. A part of me knows he is right, but I still see red flags all around what we are about to take on, and I am not so sure I am going to come out of this unchanged.

Chapter 18

"Aw damn, Tam I have been walking around with that signed contract for days. So much has been going on," Brad actually blushes.

"It's not just your contract. My boss wants to meet you, and so does my dad. It's just a little golf," I stop and shrug. "I wouldn't mind you handing over that contract, though."

I smile at him looking up through my lashes. My father called me this evening. It was hell answering all his questions about Brad. I felt like a little girl all over again. My mother is being a little more understanding. I know it is going to take some time to work on my dad.

Brad stands from his spot on the floor. Ann offered to keep Brielle for one more night. While we were able to square away the nanny and a new school for Brielle, Brad is being insistent on me helping with the house hunt. So tomorrow we will be looking for a new home.

I have to admit. The more I think about it, the more I am becoming excited about it. We are really going to do this. We are going to be a real family.

I look up at my man from my perch on the couch and lick my lips. He is barefoot in a pair of gym shorts with no shirt. His hair is loose and spilling over his broad shoulders. I can't believe I have kept my hands off him this long.

I've been behaving myself as we discuss all the things we still need to do. Then I had to find the right moment to bring up the invitation from my dad and my boss for Brad to join them for golf. Right now I want to forget it all and get lost in his body for the rest of the night.

"Tam, you're going to get in a whole lot of trouble looking at me like that," Brad says huskily. "I'm going to go get this contract before I get distracted again."

"I'm patient," I say in a silky purr as I lie back on the couch and throw my arms over my head.

Brad chuckles and shakes his head as he turns to leave. I look up at the ceiling in thought. This is not where I saw my life heading, but I can't say that I am unhappy.

"No Tiff, I'm seeing someone," I hear Brad say as he reenters the house. He rolls his eyes as he tosses the contract on the coffee table and plops down next to my feet. "Yes, it is the one from the photo. Not that it is your business."

I'm a little uncomfortable with eavesdropping on his conversation, but Brad seems fine with it. He gathers my feet in his lap and starts to massage them. I just stare at the side of his annoyed face.

"We broke up. I have a right to move on with my life. I told you I wasn't going to lie to you about her. I've always been in love with her," Brad pauses to listen.

"Why in the world would you do that?" Brad pauses in his rubbing and sits up straight. "Coming to Texas isn't going to change anything Tiff. I really think it is best if you stay away from my family and me."

I can hear her raising her voice on the other line now. It is taking everything in me not to snatch the phone from him and give this chick a piece of my mind. However, Brad beats me to it.

"Look, enough. Lose my number, Tiffany. We are done. I know you are trying to get your career back off the ground, so stalking me won't look so good if I go to the tabloids with this," Brad bites out.

He hangs up the phone putting his head back against the couch. I wait for him to calm down a bit before I climb into his lap. I put my forehead to his and start massaging his shoulders.

"Is this something I should be worried about Brad," I ask gently.

"Not at all Darlin'," he replies wrapping his strong arms around me.

"We have a daughter Brad. We have to think about her at all times. I don't want to confuse her or put her in danger. If we are going to do this, we have to do it right. I don't want her to get hurt if we don't work out," I murmur.

"As a family Tam, always as a family," he squeezes me in his arms before he stands and takes us up to my bedroom.

Chapter 19

It feels so good to have Tam open up to me. It seemed like once she did that day in the truck; I could really see us working this out. I assumed to understand the pressure Tam has in her life. However, the more she opens up, the more I understand her reluctance to be in a relationship that could tip everything she has so carefully built. It all started to make sense when I met her dad and saw how in control he is of everything at every moment.

My parents are way more laid back. I can see how much he loves Tam, though. Something tells me that he has known about me for longer than Tam thinks. She told me she never told her father who Ellie's father is, but I have a feeling he figured it out somehow. I like the man. He is blunt and to the point.

I know I can't make decisions for Tam, but I plan to do my part in making things easier for her. I've spent the last three months doing just that. After agreeing on the same school, we found a great sitter that Ann recommended. We weren't too fond of the ones we had originally set up to interview.

The sitter we chose worked out best as she happened to be the daughter of a friend of Ann's. She is also always more than willing to take Ellie to be around her cousins when they're at Ann's or my parents, which Tam and I agreed to. Ellie has been busy with dance, riding horses and sleepovers since I introduced her to my family. Tam has been in a much more peaceful place.

The media backed off since we found a place. They weren't getting much on my little family and me since Tam, and I became very cautious. They were able to place names with the faces, but that was it. I always steer them back to the team and the game. Once the season started, it got easy to deflect.

We ended up purchasing a large house; well Ranch actually, not far from my parents and my siblings. Since Tam's family is not in Texas, other than Ellerie, I thought it would be good to be surrounded by mine. Besides, the way

Tam's face lit up when we walked in the door made my heart swell. I had to buy the place for her.

The house has been just the right amount of work for us. Tam wanted a new kitchen, and I insisted she redo the master bath. All in all, we have made the place a home in a very short time. A few more weeks and upstairs will be finished and we can just enjoy it.

Things haven't changed much at work for Tamara despite our relationship and her bringing in my contract. So we have really just been settling into our new home and into our relationship. I have fallen more in love with Tam daily.

Now remember that I respect Tam's father. We get on well, but right now I am nervous to be face to face with the man. Her parents will be staying with us for a few weeks for Brielle's birthday and her party.

For a little over three months, I have fallen more and more in love with Tamara, her laugh, her smile, the cute noises she makes when I come in late at night while she is asleep or when I have to get up before her. It is like my very own greeting or her letting me know she is disappointed that I am leaving.

I love the way she gets lost in thought and when her eyes shine when she gets a great idea. I love that she runs a bath for me after home games and washes my hair and rubs my back. But if Tam did none of this I would still be in love with her, because of the way she takes care of my daughter.

I have seen loving mothers, my own mama, and my sister. However, to watch the way Tam is with Ellie makes my heart want to burst with pride. I know I am a lucky man.

Thus, the reason I am nervous today. I am not nervous to see Tam's parents. She has smoothed things over with her dad concerning me. I think our golf outing went a long way to help with that process. He and I have talked a few times since.

I guess it is not so much the face to face with her father that has me on edge. It is what I need to discuss with him that has me sweating like I'm in the fourth quarter with fifty seconds on the clock and one choice to win it all.

I wipe sweaty palms on my jeans as Tamara introduces her parents to mine. I rented this castle for Ellie's birthday to make my baby happy, but I am now hoping it shows her family how much I love my girls. I am willing to do anything to make them happy.

Tamara's mother looks around in wonder at all the decorations. There are lights and flowers everywhere. I hired every Disney princess there is. I bought little princess dresses for all of the other little girls to dress up as well. Brielle invited so many of her little friends, from her old school as well as the new one.

I couldn't leave the boys out, so I had go carts brought in to race through the gardens, and I had a little football field set up. A bunch of guys from the team showed up to help drive the kids around in the carts. Some have joined the kids on the little field to throw the ball around.

My little baby looks just like a princess in her tiara and light purple dress. Of course, the tiara is sparkling with real diamonds because I just couldn't help myself. This is only her fourth birthday. I can only imagine the mountains I will move for her wedding day.

"Pop-pop," I hear Ellie squeal as the grands get acquainted.

"There's my little princess," Byron Hathaway beams. It is the softest I have seen the man look since meeting him. It gives me hope.

"Oh Tamara, she looks adorable," Fiona, Tam's mama, gushes. "And this party, honey, you have outdone yourself with all of this."

"Oh, don't look at me," Tam laughs and points towards me. "This is all Brad. I had a much smaller party planned."

"My boy loves his girls. Nothing is too big for our Ellie," My dad beams with pride.

I feel my own pride fill my chest. I love being able to do this for my little girl. The smile on her face alone makes every penny worth it. It doesn't hurt that Tamara hasn't been able to stop smiling as well.

"Pop-pop, do you see the tiara, my daddy got for me?" Brielle coos happily.

"Yes, I do, young lady that is some tiara. Looks like your daddy has been spoiling you," Byron says good-naturedly.

"Has he," Tamara teases and looks up at me.

I wink at her and then look up at her father. "I have plenty of time to make up for. Though, I think I would spoil my girls regardless," I reply honestly.

"Vernon, Gloria, you have a fine boy here. I look forward to getting to know him some more," Byron says, with a firm nod in my direction before turning his attention back to Ellie.

"Well, I've just become the happiest woman in the world. All my favorite people in one place," Stacey squeals as she appears on the patio where food and seating are set up for everyone. She has a few other smiling faces with her.

I haven't seen Stacey since that night five years ago, but she looks pretty much the same. I am surprised when I am the first one she hugs. After an awkward moment, I hug her back.

"God, are you a sight for sore eyes," Stacey grins at me. "She is just so darn stubborn. If she wasn't my best friend I would have told you a long time ago."

"Stacey," Tamara hisses.

"What," Stacey pouts.

"Brad, this is Stacey. My crazy best friend," Tamara rolls her eyes.

"Yes, I remember her," I chuckle.

"These are my other good friends from New York," Tam offers for the other smiling faces. "This is Reese and her boyfriend, Nico. This here is Alee. And the tall guy that can't keep his eyes off the beautiful woman at his side is Uri, Nico's brother and the beauty he is staring at is Valentina, his wife. Those are their little monsters running for the go carts."

Valentina and Uri are a beautiful pair. Valentina and their children all have unusual eyes for their coloring. Valentina is chocolate with beautiful blue eyes. Their children are more caramel-skinned with blue eyes from what I get a quick glimpse of. I tilt my head to the side as I process their family.

Looking at Valentina and their children only makes me think of how unique and beautiful my own daughter is and makes me want more children with Tam. Uri murmurs something to the amused looking Valentina, and she smiles up at him. I look at Tam and smile; I wonder if we look that in love.

I haven't missed that almost all of Tam's friends are in interracial relationships, which makes me think I really did overreact all those years ago. Tamara gives me more shit about being country than being white these days. And that is always in good natured fun.

"Nice to meet you all," I say as I break out of my thoughts.

"Monroe, we may play two different footballs, but I think we can find something in common about ourselves. These ladies are about to get crazy. I think we should make a break for it now," Nico laughs as Reese slaps his arm and the other women give him the eye.

"I agree with the boy," Byron says as he steps to my side and pats me on the back.

I nod at the man I hope to call my father in law. All the men head off as the women start to talk excitedly. Uri and Nico walk ahead as they see the go carts and the other players. I plan to catch up with them in a few, but first I have some business. I look at my father who is walking in step with us and give him a nervous nod. He catches on and picks up his pace.

"Mr. Hathaway, I was hoping to get a moment alone with you," I say after clearing my throat.

"Is that right," he asks as he turns to look at me.

"Yes Sir, I was brought up in an old fashion way," I start then clear my throat. "My mama and daddy wouldn't think it right if I didn't come to you with my intentions for Tam. I know we did things a little out of order, and I know things weren't right for a long time, but I need you to know. I love your daughter more than my own life.

"I plan to do everything I can to keep my family safe happy and loved. So Sir, what I am trying to say is that I want to ask you for Tam's hand," I rush the last part out before I lose my cool.

"Son, I believe you have realized I am an observant man. My baby girl hasn't been happy for a long time, but when I look at her now, it fills my heart with joy. She has found her happiness, and I believe she has found it in you. I give you my blessing, Brad. Just remember she is my most precious gift.

"I think you understand this because Ellie has wrapped you around her finger. Just remember how precious Brielle is to you with every decision you make with her mother. Don't do anything you wouldn't want another man to do to your daughter when she is old enough to fall in love," Byron says firmly, as he stops to turn and look me in my eyes.

I nod my head a little choked up. I can only hope that Ellie finds a man that loves her as much as I love her mama.

"I've made my one mistake with Tam the night we met. I suffered for five years because of it and missed out on things I can never get back. I am all out of mistakes, Sir. I plan to treat Tamara like the queen she is," I say in all confidence.

"Well as your future father in law I will tell you this. Your competition has just arrived, and he has wanted my Tamara something fierce. I don't think he is above stepping on another man's toes either," Byron says and nods pointedly in the direction we just came from.

I turn quickly to see what he is referring to. Rage boils in my chest as a tall brown skin man pulls my woman into a hug. I clench and unclench my fists knowing it would not be a good idea to cause a scene right after asking for Tam's hand.

"That would be Mike. Nice boy but he is not looking to stop playing the field. My baby doesn't need that," Byron grunts.

"I got this," is all I say before stalking over to where my woman is standing with this Mike guy's arm draped around her shoulders.

Stacey and Reese, who are both facing me, have amused looks on their faces. One thing we don't do in Texas is touch another man's woman. This is my woman, and he is about to learn that.

I am a little uncomfortable with how aggressive Mike is being right now. I had invited him to the party months ago when we were still texting each other and going on dates here and there. I guess I should have told everyone he was no longer welcome. He had to have gotten the address from Stacey or Ellerie or something.

From his possessive hold on my shoulders, I figure he has heard about Brad. Hell, if you live in Texas it is hard not to know about Brad and me after those pictures and the speculations behind them. I tug to step out of his hold, but he just tightens his hold. I don't want to make a scene, so I grit my teeth and smile.

That's when my body starts to hum, and the hairs stand up. *Oh God, Brad, please don't make a scene,* I groan inwardly. Suddenly large muscular arms are wrapped around my waist pulling my back into his chest and out of Mike's hold. Brad's hand comes up, cupping my face and turning it up to his.

His full lips crush mine, taking them in a passionate and possessive kiss. I am stunned as my brain short circuits, and I melt into his arms. When he breaks the kiss, his blue eyes are sparkling with lust and mischief as he stares back at me.

I hear giggles and chuckles behind us and turn to see my mother smiling happily. Reese raises a brow and her glass at Brad. My eyes land on Mike, and he is fuming as he takes in Brad from head to toe.

"Damn," Stacey snorts.

"Exactly," Valentina mutters.

"I like him," Reese laughs.

Mike looks like he is about to make his own comment when Brielle comes flying over out of nowhere. "Daddy," she squeals happily. She runs right into Brad's leg. "Daddy, you promised to drive me in a go cart. I want to race Nori; his daddy is going to drive him."

"I'll drive you," Mike says with a smug smile on his face.

I want to smack the smile right off. The whole time we dated he tried to use Ellie to get his way on just about everything. I see my mother and the girls frowning as well out the corner of my eyes.

"Hey, Mr. Mike," Ellie chirps. "Thank you, but I want my Daddy to drive me."

"Your daddy is ready to, Sugar," Brad says with a cocky grin on his face. "Let's go win us a race."

"I'll keep Tam company for you big man," Mike says smugly.

"Ellie baby, you go pick us out a car," Brad says pushing Ellie toward the cars.

"Okay," she sings and takes off as fast as her little legs will take her.

"I don't think we have met properly. I'm Bradley Monroe, Tam's man, and Ellie's father. I don't share what's mine, so unless I'm misreading your body language you might want to check yourself around my family," Brad growls low.

"Where were you when I was taking care of your family," Mike hissed back.

My head whips back and I turn to glare at Mike. Brad goes to lunge at him, but I place my body between them, placing a hand on Brad's chest. "I don't remember you taking care of anything Mike," I snap. "We dated for a while, nothing more. Just dates. Don't try to play me or my man like I'm some

241

cheap hoe or something, especially in front of my family. I think you should leave."

"Come on Tam, it's not like that, and you know it," Mike sighs in frustration.

"Nah man," my brother rumbles as he steps up beside Brad. "You're my boy, but I'm not feeling what you're trying right now. This man asked you to respect his family, and my sister asked you to leave. You told me you didn't want any trouble. You wanted to come for Ellie. That's not looking to be true to me right now, so I'm feeling some type of way. I think you should take all of our suggestions and make a quick exit."

"Yeah, alright man," Mike nods but doesn't look to happy about conceding.

We all watch him walk off. I look up at Brad to see his jaw working under the skin. I wasn't expecting him to claim his position so firmly. Honestly, my panties are soaked right now. Brad is hot when he is protecting what is his.

His blue eyes are blazing, and his cheeks are flushed red from anger. I bite back a laugh because, in this very moment, my man is looking like Thor, ready to go into battle. I lift up on my toes and wrap my arms around his neck.

"Bradley," I call his name as he is still watching Mike leave. "Baby," I call again.

This time, his eyes slowly meet mine. I reach to tuck his hair behind his ear and cup his face with my hand. "Thank you for defending me, but he isn't worth being upset over. Our baby is waiting on you. She is excited for her daddy to win her a race. Last thing we want is for you to be like this while driving our daughter around at her party," I say softly.

He pinches his eyes closed and when they open again the storm that was brewing is gone. He tugs on my waist and brings his lips down on mine in a passionate kiss before pulling away and placing a kiss to my forehead. He doesn't say another word as he turns and heads for an excited Bri.

I stand watching my man walk over to our daughter scooping her up and tossing her in the air before he catches her, whispering something in her ear that causes her to throw her head back and laugh. He then walks over to Uri and his son, shaking hands with Uri as Bri shakes hands with Nori. Then they are off into their go carts.

"You know my husband will take care of that little problem for you," Valentina says with a sly smile. I have come to know this woman and her husband through her brother in law and Reese in the last four years. They have secrets, and I know from Reese that they are nothing nice.

She may be smiling and looking amused as she says this, but I know that the teasing tone she is using is in case someone else hears. Reese steps to my other side shaking her head. "Behave Valentina," Reese chuckles. "Although, I told you there was something I never liked about him. He was trying to get a beat down today. If looks could kill, with the way your father, Nico, and Uri were looking over here that man would be toast."

"I'm just saying we can make that happen," Valentina shrugs. "How is he going to come to this baby's party disrespecting not just you but her father as well?"

Valentina places a hand on her hip and presses her lips. "Ignore her," Reese giggles, she has been extra snippy since we got on the plane.

"Mama," Valentina's daughter Vita runs up and rifles off rapid Italian to her mother excitedly.

"Vita baby, English, what have I told you," Valentina says gently.

"Mama, Uncle Nico promised Inzo he would drive him around the track. I want to race too, Mama. Will you drive me please?" the precious little girl asks her mother.

"Oh honey, I don't think that is a good idea for mommy right now. Remember we talked about this," Valentina says.

"Oh," Vita says sadly then places a hand on her mother's stomach. She kisses her mother's belly and pats it. "I forgot."

"You're pregnant again," Reese gasps. It is hard to miss the sadness in her eyes. "I should have known, that explains."

Valentina groans. "Nico asked us not to tell you yet," Valentina sighs.

"Why does he do that," Reese says, almost in a whisper to herself.

Alee moves in to wrap an arm around Reese. "Because he loves you and it has torn him up watching you go through the same thing over and over. When are you going to accept what you two have? Accept his proposal." Alee encourages.

"We are not here to talk about me. We are here to have fun and celebrate Brielle," Reese huffs.

"That may be so, but we are going to talk about the elephant in the room soon," I say.

"My story will finish itself when it is ready. Now back to you. That man is in love with you. How are things going? You look so happy," Reese says to me.

"I can't complain things have been perfect, almost too perfect. I can't help but think that there is a shoe somewhere waiting to drop," I bite my lip. "It was such a big step to move in together, but I have never been happier, and neither has Brielle. She adores her father. I just don't want her to get attached, and things blow up in her face."

"Blow up in her face or yours," Reese asks as she tilts her head at me.

"It sounds to me like you are the one that is afraid to get attached," Stacey adds in. I knew she wasn't going to be quiet much longer.

"I think it is a bit late for that," I groan. "I crave that man something fierce, and I would be lying if I said that hasn't always been the case."

"Then let yourself be happy for once without looking over your shoulder," Stacey says, wrapping an arm around my shoulders and squeezing. She then looks at Reese. "That goes for you too, because I would fuck your man in a heartbeat. Phew."

"*Stacey,*" Reese draws out. "If I didn't know you from childhood you would come up missing one of these days."

"All jokes aside, you know I am right," Stacey says pointedly.

"Oh, don't worry, if Nico is anything like his brother, she is only on borrowed time. He will wait for so much longer before he gives her no way out," Valentina says with a sly smile on her lips.

"Whatever," Reese mutters. "Come on Vita. I'll drive you."

"Truth hurts," Alee speaks up.

"I don't think I can blame her," I say as I watch my friend walk away.

"Oh no honey, I was talking about you. It hurts to see how much that man really loves you and yet you are still trying to find reasons why you should run," Alee says knowingly.

"When are you heifers flying out again," I grumble and head off after Reese and Vita. I can hear them cackling behind me.

Chapter 20

The party was a huge success. I got to spend some time with my girls, my baby had the time of her life, and my man put on display what Brielle and I mean to him for everyone to see. I couldn't have asked for anything more, but some of the things the girls said have been playing in my head all evening, almost to the point of distraction.

I guess that's why I have found myself wondering where everyone has gone. One minute the girls were all helping me gather gifts the next I am looking around and everyone is gone. I had been in deep thought about the speech Brad gave as we cut the cake.

"Thank you, everyone, for coming out to share our little girl's day. I have come home to Texas to find that my world has been here all along. The things I thought I couldn't live without are no longer a priority to me, because what I can't live without are my two girls.

"I find myself to be a lucky man, and as soon as she'll have me, I plan to lock down my future with the woman I love more than life itself. I want to create more beautiful little girls, and some handsome boys," everyone laughs at that last remark and Brad kisses Brielle's cheek as he holds her in his arms and then pulls me closer to kiss the top of my head. *"So thank you all again for making this a wonderful and special day for my family."*

I was left stunned by his speech. I have gotten over taking things slow with Brad, but that doesn't mean his words didn't shock me a little. We have gotten so close in the last few months. He knows me better than most people in my life. It is like our bodies, minds and souls have become one and in sync with one another.

Truthfully, these days when I try to find a reason that we shouldn't be together I come up empty handed. Brad has really stepped things up. He may make little mistakes here and there, like letting Bri manipulate him without checking with me first. But I can't fault him for that. He spoils us both as much as I will allow him and it comes from his heart.

The man breathes to see us happy. That in itself brings a smile to my face. I never knew I wanted to be cherished this way until Brad started to show me just what I really want in a relationship. I never thought about it before because it wasn't a priority, now it is like second nature to want to be loved the way I know only Brad can love me.

I look around and wrinkle my brows. *How did I not see everyone leave?* The lights have even grown dim. *Where is everyone? Was I really that deep in thought?* I spin in a circle, and my brows draw in deeper.

Suddenly, soft pink and red lights come up giving the gardens a soft romantic glow. I laugh to myself. This must be the staff's way of telling us it is time for us to go. I turn back to the bag of gifts I had been filling, but the air fills with music. I look around confused at first.

When I realize that they are playing a country version of *Falling Slowly.* I laugh to myself. I can't tell you how many times I have heard a country version of a song I like, since moving here to Texas. I shrug and turn back to the bag once again, but this time, I stop as I see Brad standing with a white rose between his teeth and a small white and grey Pitbull in his arms.

Brielle has been hounding him for a dog for weeks since seeing the puppies one of the dogs at the ranch gave birth to. I eye the dog warily but burst out laughing when the puppy actually looks like he is pleading with me with his big blue eyes, just like the man that is holding him is doing.

"What are you up to?" I say with a smile. "I thought we agreed that Bri would get a puppy when she could care for it. Like in six or seven years from now," I chide.

Brad pulls the rose from his mouth and hands it to me. "Yeah, well, I started to think about how often I'll be leaving my girls without me, and this little guy started to sound like a good idea," Brad shrugs.

The puppy is adorable. As Brad scratches his neck around the collar while talking to me, the puppy looks between the two of us. He is so cute. I don't have the heart to be upset or to deny wanting to keep him.

"Will you dance with us," Brad asks with a little boyish grin on his lips.

How can I resist? I throw my head back and laugh as Brad steps closer to me. I wrap my arms around his waist and place my head on his chest. When he wraps the arm holding the puppy around me the little pup starts to push his little cold nose into my back and paw at me.

"Easy Six, we want her to like you," Brad says to the dog.

I laugh again. "Six?" I lift my head to look at him and lift a brow. "Why in the world have you named the dog Six?"

"It was my number when I met you," Brad says with a smile. "I won a ring with it. I figured it would bring me luck tonight."

My brows draw together, and I give him a curious look. "Why would you need luck tonight?"

"This song, it says what I don't know how to say about the night I met you. I saw you and even though I didn't know you I wanted you. I let silly words fool me, and I didn't know how to react to you then. You have pointed me home again Tam.

"I have found where I want to be for the rest of my life. I can be content on our ranch with our children and our dog as long as I have you there with me. What I am saying is that I am hoping that Six here brings me luck because," Brad pauses and releases me as he gets down on one knee.

I lift a shaky hand to my lips as they part in shock. Brad lifts the puppy up toward me, and I notice for the first time that there is a huge rock dangling from his collar. "I want to ask you to marry me, Tamara. I don't want anyone else. You are it for me. I want you and Ellie to finally have my last name," Brad says, as his eyes blaze with the love I know he has for me.

"If I say no do I get to keep the puppy," I tease as tears leak from my eyes.

"Tam," Brad growls.

"Yes, of course, I'll marry you," I laugh.

Cheers and hand claps come from out of nowhere, and our family starts to pour out of their hiding places. Even my friends are here for this. I can't believe he planned all this without me knowing. I mean Bri can't hold water.

"We have a puppy mommy," Bri squeals excitedly, as she runs up and throws her arms around her father's neck as he releases the string that has the ring attached to Six's collar.

"Yes, we do," I say as I give Brad the eye.

"Good boy," Brad coos to the dog as he pets his head and grins widely at me. He hands Bri the puppy and pulls me to him for a searing kiss before placing the huge diamond ring on my finger. Once the ring is on my finger the weight of it brings me to reality.

I just agreed to marry this man. He is going to be mine for the rest of my life. I almost want to pinch myself. Somehow I think our trial has really just begun.

Everyone gathers around to congratulate us and get a look at the ring. I don't miss the sour look on Donna's face as she stands off to the side. Whatever her problem is she can shove it. I won't let anything ruin this moment for me.

Chapter 21

"Really Gloria, you and Vernon didn't have to go through all this trouble," Tam says to my mama. It is the night of our engagement party.

Let's just say that my parents have gone ahead and done it Texas style. Tam has been nervous all day. I may have gone big with Ellie's birthday party, but that was a mix of my family but mostly Tamara's family and friends. This engagement party is going to triple in size. My mama has called in the cavalry. Family I haven't even seen in years.

"Oh, nonsense, I can't have my baby boy find the love of his life and not celebrate that with everyone that is important.

This was no trouble at all," my mama replies. "Now let me get a look at you. You look absolutely lovely, honey."

My mama is right; I haven't been able to take my eyes off my fiancée. Tamara took my breath away the moment she came down the stairs in the Ivory dress she has on. It has thin straps and is cut into a tasteful v down the front. The dress is fitted in the top, showing off her slim waist and the silky skirts flare out at the waist stopping just above the knee to show off her amazing legs.

Her pretty feet are encased in a pair of navy blue heels with her cute red toes peeking out, just adding to her sexy legs. Her hair is brushed up into a neat soft bun; that is elegant messy as she called it. The studs in her ears only add to the elegance of her look.

Her chocolate skin is glowing against the silky fabric of her dress. I have imagined passing my tongue across her collarbone a few times. I'm honored to have her at my side, even if I am the complete opposite in contrast to her city elegance. I cleaned up pretty well for tonight. I opted for a pair of blue jeans and a white button-down shirt with a dark navy blue sports jacket. Just because I know my woman would get a kick out of it, I have worn cowboy boots and a cowboy hat as well.

I love the smile that spread across her face as I placed the hat on my head when we went to leave the house. Tam can tease me about my country ass all she wants, but she loves this country boy right down to my cowboy boots.

"Thank you, Gloria, you look beautiful as always, and this place looks amazing," Tam tells my mama as she takes in the tent that has been set up in the backyard at the family ranch.

The subtle pinks, blues and purples have the place looking that right amount of both feminine and masculine. I heard Ann gushing to Tam that it was all to be country chic. Whatever they want to call it, my mama and sister have outdone themselves. From the smile on my woman's face, I know she loves and appreciates it. I can't tell you how much it warms my heart that Tam and my family get along so well. They really love her.

Tam and my father have even gone riding together a few times. I have to say I am a little jealous on that front. I have been so busy with the season that I haven't had much time to get out to the ranch for a ride yet. Little does Tam know, but my father has a beautiful mare for her as an engagement gift.

She is going to love her. Daddy spent weeks looking for just the right horse for her. Ellie has been so busy with the new puppy at the house she hasn't been to the ranch in a few weeks, which allowed us to keep Tam's horse a secret. I love my little girl, but if she gets wind of something, then everyone is going to know about it.

That's why I have kept my own surprises to myself. I hadn't told Ellie about the puppy at her birthday party until the absolute last minute. I plan to hit Tam with the big gifts tonight. She has pleaded with me not to go overboard, and I think the only reason she gave in on having such a large engagement party is because I caved on the size of the wedding.

I wanted to go all out and spoil her, but she wasn't having it. There will be no princess castle and horse drawn buggy for my bride. Well, the jury is still out on the horse drawn buggy. I think I may be wearing her down on that one. No matter how small she wants the wedding I still intend on making sure she feels like a princess, but as I look around again, I can see why she bulked at the huge wedding her mama and mine were in the midst of planning at first.

I can tell you I really caved because she promised me a baby. I'm still grinning like a lunatic, and it has been weeks since she promised that we'd start to expand our family sooner rather than later. I haven't gotten a clear answer on what that timeline really means, but it is something when it comes to Tam. She had flat out told me no many times before.

"Oh my God, a projector, oh Gloria please tell me you and mother haven't been going through old picture of me. You two do want Brad to marry me right," Tam teases.

I wrap an arm around her waist and pull her into my chest. "There is nothing they can show me that will stop me from marrying you," I murmur against her neck.

"You haven't seen me in braces," Tam grumbles, and I laugh.

"Actually Darlin', I have. Your daddy keeps a picture of you back then in his wallet. He showed it to me on the golf course the first time we met," I laugh louder when her face compresses in horror.

"No, he wouldn't," she gasps.

"Yeah, he did," I chuckle.

"Oh Daddy," she groans into her hands. "Come on."

"You were adorable, Baby," I give her a squeeze and her head lifts to look me in the eyes.

"You know it is not good to lie to your future wife," Tam says placing a hand on her hip, but she has an adorable smile on her lips.

"That's why I never do," I smile back at her.

"You two are just so sweet to watch. I couldn't have asked for a better match for my son," My mama says wiping at her eyes.

"Come here," I say pulling her into a hug with us and kissing her cheek. "I always wanted a woman as sweet as you, and I got lucky."

"You got better than lucky," my mother says cupping Tam's face. "Now where in the world is my grandbaby. She called me a million times today about this party."

Tam throws her head back and laughs. "Well, she ran into Jess when we got out the car and took off with her. I don't think we will be seeing her for the rest of the night unless we look for Jess."

"I swear I am about to nickname that little one shadow," Mama laughs. "Her little heart is going to be broken when Trev lets Jess get serious about boys."

I splay my hand on Tam's belly. "Well, hopefully by then we will have given her a brother or sister of her own," I say with a wide grin.

"Bradley," Tam elbows me.

"Oh please honey. This boy has been talking about another baby since he found out he was a father. I thought his father was going to have to hog-tie him to keep him out of your house until you were ready to see where things would go," my mama chortles.

"Really Brad," Tam looks up at me with her mouth open.

I shrug and give her a boyish grin. "What?"

Tam just shakes her head and laughs. "Well, it looks like guests are starting to arrive. Let's get you two in place to greet them," Mama says as she starts to push us along.

I happily lead my fiancée to the front of the tent to greet our guests. I am in anticipation for a great night tonight. At least, I think I am.

~B~

Thank God I made it clear that I don't want a huge wedding. This engagement party is so over the top, and to think they put it together in just two months. Between all of the food and all of the people, you would think this was some type of party at the White House. Don't get me wrong, I am so grateful to Vernon and Gloria for putting this all together but goodness. I know my mother had a hand in this as well.

I have cousins here I haven't seen since I was like nine. There is only one important face that is missing, but her other half is here. I think Nico showed up in hopes that Reese would make an appearance. Sadly, she hasn't reached out to me, and I don't know how to help.

That is just one of the many things that are on my mind tonight. I have been really cautious about letting Brad know what I think is going on. It could be me and my imagination going wild, but I lost three clients this week. Three of my sports clients at that, I have been close with all three so it came as a shock to find out that they dropped me as their lawyer and won't return my calls.

For one client, Kelley, I was actually in the middle of some major negotiations for him. I go above and beyond for my clients. I get them things not even their agents can deliver on. I have never lost a client. If anything, they always bring in more business.

Since Brad announced our engagement, I have been getting mixed reactions when I attend his games and hang out in the box seats he provides. A few times I have chosen to sit with friends in their boxes when they offer, just to avoid the team box, with the wives and other team royalty. I would never say any of this to Brad. He is having a great season, and I don't want this on his shoulders. It is bad enough he refuses to wait until after the football season is done altogether to get married.

When, not if, his team makes it to the playoffs our wedding weekend is going to be chaos, which is another reason I opted for a small wedding. I want him to have the least amount of stress possible. He and Ellerie are really making it happen on the field, and I don't want to be the cause for that to change, so I have said nothing about all of this.

That doesn't mean that my suspicions have disappeared. Cyrus has continued to let me know he has my back. Honestly, the thought has crossed my mind repeatedly. I've thought about running my suspicions all by Cyrus, but he has been out of town for a few weeks, although he promised he would be back in time for this engagement party.

I wouldn't bring up any of my suspicions at this event, though. So here I stand with a smile on my face like nothing is really on my mind. When I feel like I am holding the weight of the world. A part of me wants to believe that Stacey and the girls are right. I am just looking for the other shoe to drop. But in my gut, I know better.

"Where are you," Brad leans to whisper in my ear.

After greeting guests at the opening of the tent for an hour, we made our way to our table for dinner. Everything was delicious and in no time Brad and I were both being embarrassed with speeches from our family and close friends. I was really embarrassed when Brad gave me a ridiculously expensive diamond necklace in front of everyone. It didn't stop there. His dad gave me a horse and Brad decided the necklace and horse were not enough, so he handed over the key to a Maserati I had my eye on for a little while now.

If I didn't know that I could afford any of these gifts without the help of Brad, I would have felt some type of way to receive such gifts in front of all these people. As it is, I feel like some of the people that don't know any different are judging me.

We are now moving around the tent to greet whoever we missed in the beginning. I have drifted off into thought a few times, but I hadn't realized that Brad noticed. I need to get it together.

"I'm here," I say as I join the room from my thoughts. "I was just thinking about how amazing the night has turned out."

"You sure, because you looked like you were somewhere deeper than that. You're not having second thoughts about me are you?" He says this teasingly, but the look in his eyes tells me that he is only half joking.

I place my champagne glass on a passing tray before wrapping my arms around his neck. "I have not had one, second thought since I said yes," I say and peck his lips. "Well, except for when you put that cowboy hat on this evening," I tease.

"Oh really, is that right because I do believe I saw your eyes light up. I was thinking I would get you and Ellie matching hats, and we could go to the rodeo as one big happy family," he smirks at me.

I love this man. Does he even know how much? I'm thrown back to the night we met and the easy banter we had while he made me laugh. To think I was trying to pawn him off on someone else.

"While I think Bri would love that, I think you will have a much tougher sell with me," I smile up at him.

"I'm going to make a country girl out of you yet," he murmurs against my lips before pressing in for a tender kiss. "I love you."

"Funny, I was thinking the same thing about you," I whisper back, breathless from the simple kiss.

"Bradley, I hate to interrupt, but I have someone here that wanted to say hello," Donna's annoying voice cuts through our moment. I just bet she didn't want to interrupt.

Brad releases his hold on my waist and places his hand on the small of my back before turning. When he gets a look at the woman standing with Donna, he stiffens, and the smile falls from his face. I am instantly on alert. I look this woman over with her platinum blonde hair and tight bandage dress. I know she looks familiar. When a camera flashes from somewhere nearby, I know exactly where I know her from. This is his ex-girlfriend, what was her name, Tiffany. You have got to be kidding me.

Why is his supermodel ex at our engagement party? I glare at Donna, from the smug look on her face, she knows exactly who this is and how inappropriate this is. It is taking everything in me not to slap the piss out of her right now. We usually stay clear of each other, because the feeling of dislike is mutual.

It looks like today this heifer wants to turn things up a notch. Before I can say a word, to my surprise, Brad grabs Tiffany and storms off with her in tow. I am stunned, and a bit hurt. I blink a few times to make sure this is really happening.

"Guess you don't have this one as locked up as you thought," Donna snarls.

"What is your damn problem," I hiss back at her.

"You are. You come in here with your little brat. She is so cute, and everyone is falling all over themselves to please her and you. You have no right to be here," she says with venom dripping from her words.

"I have no right to be here," I scoff. "By whose rules?"

"Oh come on honey, you aren't stupid. Name one star football player with a black wife. Name one quarterback…

name an open relationship between a white player and his black plaything.

"Didn't think so. You see honey that is all you are, a plaything. When Brad gets tired of playing house with you, he is going to find himself the right kind of woman to be by his side, a woman that will fit into his world. Nope, you and that brat won't be around long at all, especially when he remembers how good he had it before you," Donna finishes with a nasty grin on her face.

I refuse to let her words sting me. I won't allow her to plant this poison. Not tonight of all nights. I have always known Donna disliked me. A large part of me has suspected that my color plays a part in it, but this confirms it all. I stand up taller and narrow my eyes at her.

"Last time I checked Brad, and I could care less what other people do. Who cares? Our relationship has nothing to do with his game on the field," I snap. "If you have a problem with me and my daughter then that is on you. But I will tell you this…call my daughter, a name again, and you will find out what a plaything is because I'm going to whip your ass like a ragdoll."

I turn and walk away from a stunned looking Donna. I look around the crowded tent for my fiancé, but I don't see him or the woman he stormed off with. I refuse to acknowledge the tears burning the backs of my eyes because that means I will have to acknowledge the fact that some of her words did get to me.

"Hey Tam, there you are," Ann says cheerfully. "Mama has been looking for you and Brad. They want to start the presentation. Where's Brad?"

"I have no idea," I say more bitterly than I mean to.

"Is everything okay," Ann asks looking confused and concerned.

"I don't even know right now," I huff and pinch the bridge of my nose. Ann grabs my hand and pulls me off to the side away from prying ears.

"Okay, spill, what is going on," Ann demands. I need to vent to someone.

~B~

"What the hell are you doing here?" I growl at Tiffany once I have pulled her from the tent.

She pouts at me and moves closer to rub her hand up and down my arm. I snatch my arm away and cross my arms over my chest. I can't believe she is here. I have been avoiding her calls and even blocked her number a few times as she has started to call from different numbers.

I have never invited her to meet my family, so I have no idea why she would even be here now. How the hell does she know about tonight? We may have invited a lot of people, but it was made clear this was a private event for Tam and me. We didn't want the press getting wind and ruining things. I have a million thoughts running through my head, and I need answers.

"Aren't you happy to see me?" she purrs.

"No," I hiss.

"Oh come on Brad. We were so good together. Why are you being like this? You can't really be in love with this woman. Not after the chemistry, we had," Tiffany coos as if she has lost her mind. She must have.

"I don't know what chemistry you are talking about. Maybe we were in two different relationships because I told you from the start I wasn't into it. You pushed for more and I gave you the only thing you were going to get. We are over

271

and have been way before I got together with my fiancée," I snarl at her.

"Oh please Brad, she will never fit into your world, and you know it. We, on the other hand, fit together. With you on your way to the super bowl and my new movie coming out we can really give this a go and make so much happen for both our careers," she says with an enthusiastic look on her face.

I groan internally. Was she always this out of it and I just ignored it? I can't believe she is this delusional. I couldn't get rid of her things from my place fast enough. I made it pretty clear back then that it was over. What the fuck is she rambling about right now?

"Look Tiff, I don't know if you are on something or not but you have lost your mind if you think I am leaving my woman to be some publicity stunt for you and your career. I want you gone. How the hell did you get in, in the first place? It was by invitation only," I narrow my eyes at her with my last question.

"I came as Collen's plus one," she says with a smug smile that I want to slap off her face. If my mama didn't teach me better, I would.

I can't believe that bitch Donna. Collen is her little brother. There is no way he met up with Tiffany on his own. He is barely a kid. This has Donna written all over it. I plan to have it out with my brother's wife once and for all. I warned her about messing with my family.

I am fuming. I know I need to get back inside to my woman. Tiffany is just staring at me with crazy eyes. I pull my cell phone from my pocket and text security to come and collect her. I want to watch her be removed from the premises. I plan to have a restraining order filed first thing Monday. Tam was right, we have a little girl to protect. I won't let any harm come to my woman or my child.

"Brad, can't we work things out," Tiffany asks sweetly, just as security walks up behind her. I nod my head at them, and she turns to notice the two broad men ready to escort her off the premises. "Oh my God Brad, seriously? We have been friends for so long. Are you really going to throw me out?"

"See that she leaves the property and does not come back," I snap.

~B~

"He just took off with her and said nothing to me," I finish in a hushed whisper to Ann.

273

Ann opens her mouth as if to say something but closes it quickly. I freeze as large arms wrap around my waist. "Mama wants us up front," Brad says with no explanation of where he has been. I turn in his arms and glare at him. "We'll talk about it. I just don't want to ruin the night."

I just nod and follow him as he leads us to where the rest of the family has gathered. Donna is there with a smug smile on her face once again, as she clings to Trevor. He looks none too pleased with her as usual. Brad steers us clear of them, but I can feel tension rolling off of him. I'm not sure what to think about it.

Ann stands between Sam and Trevor and whispers something to Trevor that makes him frown and snatch his arm from Donna's hold as he turns to glare at her. The stupid smile on her face melts a little as panic starts to rise in her eyes. Trevor puts as much distance between them as he can without making a scene.

I am pulled from watching their interaction by Bradley squeezing my hand. I look up at him, and he gives me a weak smile before placing a kiss to my lips. Vernon and Gloria join us with Brielle hanging from her grandfather's hip. He is telling her something that has her quite amused as she giggles in his arms.

"Okay, everybody," the DJ calls out. "It looks like we have the whole family here now. I'm getting the head nod that we can start this little show."

The projector lights up, and I feel myself relax as pictures of Brad as a little boy come up on the screen. Everyone aws and ahs at the pictures and then a few of my baby pictures come up pulling the same reaction. I smile when my pictures are followed by Brielle's. I love that they have included her in this moment. When Ann asked me for Brielle's pictures I had no idea, it was for this.

The crowd roars with laughter as a picture of the three of us hits the screen. Brad and Brielle are making silly faces at me, and I am laughing to the point of tears. I remember that day. We were all at dinner over Ann's. It is just dawning on me how much time we spend with Ann and her family. I have really taken these people in as family, which means Bri is as attached as I am.

This fact stings as uncertainty tries to creep in. Looking at the three of us, we look like the perfectly happy family, but how long will that last? What am I signing up to put my daughter through? I could forgive Brad for breaking my heart, but never for breaking Brielle's. She loves her father so much.

As my thoughts start to stray, the pictures disappear from the screen bringing me back from my reverie. I look around to see the confused faces of Ann and Gloria. A rumbling voice rings out through the room instead of the soft music that had been playing with the video.

It's Brad's voice. I could never mistake his voice. I look to the screen to see him shirtless lying in bed. At first, he is all you can see and hear, but then a female voice joins in.

"Babe, do you love me," the woman says.

"Of course, I do," Brad says in return.

Tiffany comes into view as she lays her head on his shoulder. "It will be just like you promised. We will always be together. Nothing can keep us apart," Tiffany says while looking up at him longingly.

"Yeah baby, just like I promised. No matter what, I will always come back to you. This is only temporary. When I get my head cleared, we will be together. I just need some time, but you know I have never loved anyone the way I love you...."

The rest of his words are lost on me. Brad and Trevor both have run to the projector trying to cut it off. I can hear Brad shouting. "Turn that fucking thing off."

It doesn't matter. I have heard enough and so has everyone in this room. I feel stupid and embarrassed beyond belief. Brad told me he never loved her. I remember asking him. I remember his words, but the words on that screen tell me something else.

Brad is a liar. I am barely holding onto the tears that are threatening to spill over. I back away from everyone, ignoring Vernon and Gloria calling my name and start to run. I don't know where I am running to, I just run.

I can't breathe. Why is this happening to me? I finally have to admit to myself how much I have really wanted this with Brad. However, I have not signed up to be humiliated or to ruin my career. I have been so stupid in really thinking about changing my life for him.

I choke on a sob as I think about how I was considering being a stay at home mom and giving Brad the baby he has been asking for sooner, rather than later. I often regret the time I have missed with Brielle as I have built my career over the last four years. Even without Brad, I could afford to take a break. I just thought it would be better to do it with him and for our family.

This ranch is huge and Brad drove so I don't have keys to just take off. I know Bri is in good hands. When I get far away from here I'll text Ellerie to drop her off to me once I find a hotel to stay in. We rented out my old place just last month. Maybe my parents will take Brielle for a few days while I figure things out.

I look around frustrated and see the stables. Thinking of the horse Vernon gifted me with this evening; I head there. I snort as I think of the car Brad gave me. I would take off in it, but it is blocked in by everyone else.

I slip into the stable, and the calm of the horses grounds me. I head straight to Autumn, my new horse. I see a blanket outside her stall and reach for it as it has gotten cooler out. The tent for the party itself was actually heated. I wrap myself in the blanket and lean my head against Autumn's, as I pet the side of her head. She is such a sweet horse.

"What do I do, Autumn?" I whisper. "I have never been so hurt. All of his promises mean nothing because he lied."

I don't know how much time goes by while I continue to plea with Autumn for answers she will never give me. I haven't been able to stop the tears that started the moment I realized she wouldn't be answering me and that I still don't know how I got here.

I feel him in the stable with me before I see him. I look for the nearest exit, but I am too late. He wraps his arms around me and buries his face into my hair. In that moment, I shatter. This is home for me, what do you do when your home is taken from you?

~B~

I have looked all over for Tam. I had come into the stable to grab a horse to broaden my search and cover more land. I have no idea why I didn't think to look here first. My head is still too messed up at the thought that Tiffany and Donna would go so far to ruin my engagement party.

That video was not what it looked like, but I know that it looked a certain way to Tam and our hundreds of guests. This is all on me. I let my family down once again, but I won't lose my woman over this. I can't.

"Tam, baby, you have to listen to me," I say gently into her hair.

She spins in my arms, and my heart breaks even more as I see the tears soaking her face. I never want to see my baby hurting. I love this woman with everything that I am. I go to cup her face, but she pulls away. I place my hands on the stall behind her and bend to place my forehead to hers as my own tears form.

"You hurt me," she chokes out. "How could you lie to me like that?"

"I have never lied to you," I say as my own tears start to fall. I have never cried like this, but with Tam, I feel everything in the depths of my heart. This lie that I have no control over has hurt her, but it is not a lie I have told.

She scoffs and turns her face away from me. I press my forehead to the side of her face and move my arms to wrap around her. She struggles at first, but I tighten my hold.

"Just leave me alone," she whimpers.

"I can't. I love you. I would never lie to you Darlin', I swear it," I respond.

"You told me you didn't love her. You said you never had those types of feelings for her. You said you made that clear to her. So what didn't you lie about Brad? Because that video made it clear about everything you did lie about," she snaps.

I cup her face and turn it, forcing her to look up at me. "I never loved her, and that tape proves nothing. I told you

Tiffany was into acting. She would come to my place and ask me to rehearse lines with her. A few times she taped it. She said she wanted to watch the videos back to see what she could improve on.

"I never saw any harm in it back then. I had no idea she would try to use the footage against me. Baby, that was a skit from a movie she was trying to get a part in. We had been at it for hours. I was tired from practice and she pounced and begged for me to help her as soon as I crawled into bed for a nap.

"I knew those lines by heart by the time she started to tape. That was not a conversation between lovers. It was a boyfriend helping his girlfriend run lines. You are the woman I love," I place a gentle kiss to her lips. "You are the only woman I want. I have never lied to you Tamara, and I don't plan on starting now. I have a buddy that actually worked that audition. I plan to call him and see if he can send me the script and Tiffany's audition tape so that you can see I'm telling the truth."

She eyes me warily as her tears continue to fall. I move my hands to her waist and pull her to me, kissing her passionately, trying to show her how I feel with my lips. To my relief, she doesn't pull away. Her arms lock around my neck and I groan in relief.

I need to make her understand what she means to me. I pull away and hold a finger up. I pull my phone out to text Trevor to let everyone know I have found her, and then I text security to have them make sure we are not disturbed in this barn.

I tuck my phone away and reach for her hand. I pull her along down a few stalls to an empty one. I grab one of the blankets we keep in the stable. Once inside the stall, I lay out the blanket before lowering to it and tugging Tam down into my lap. She straddles my hips, and I cup her face.

"I love you, Tam," I say as I swipe at her tears. I place a soft kiss to her trembling lips. "You are everything to me."

I kiss her again to fuse my words into her brain. I place my forehead to hers as my hands make their way slowly down her face, to her throat, letting my fingertips trail across her collarbone. I feel her shiver and go to pull the blanket she is wrapped in tighter around her, but she shrugs out of the blanket and scoots forward in my lap. Her arms wrap my head, her fingers diving into my hair as her lips meet mine. I groan as I taste our tears mixed together.

I reach to continue my exploration of her body. I run my fingers across her shoulders catching the straps to her dress and pulling them with me as I move my fingers down her arms. I gently move one hand to the zipper at the back of her dress and release it nice and slow. I want her to have time to process each touch and what I am conveying with each one.

"I won't stop loving you, Baby. I can't live without you. Not again," I breathe in her ear, and she shivers once again.

I unclasp her bra and unhurriedly peel it and her dress down. Gently I tilt her body back and peel the dress from her body, bringing her panties with it. I just stare at my woman lying before me naked, except for her heels, splayed wide open for me.

I trail my fingertips up her calves to her thighs. I squeeze her upper thigh and drag her body closer to mine. I capture her bottom lip and pull it between my teeth. Tam takes her time pushing my blazer from my shoulders. I have set the tone. We are going to take this nice and slow.

I push my tongue into her mouth for a devouring deep kiss. Meanwhile, she works the buttons of my shirt before pushing it too from my shoulders. When I release her mouth to kiss her neck, she buries her face in my neck and starts to suck at the sensitive flesh. I groan and rock my hips up, brushing her hot pussy with my jean covered erection.

"You turn me on so much, Baby," I groan in her ear, and she whimpers.

"Brad," she gasps as I palm her breasts and roll her nipples between my fingertips.

"I'm so in love with you, Tam. Do you understand that," I whisper in her ear then lick it before sucking on her lobe.

Tam reaches to free me from my jeans, and I lift my hips to help as I toe off my boots. As my hands make a slow accession up her sides, my lips caress her skin, making a trip to her breasts. I kiss each one before pulling her hardened left nipple into my mouth. I know it is her more sensitive one.

To prove my point, she trembles and cries out, arching her back into me. My cock twitches against her stomach, and she takes it as an invitation. Tam reaches for me and lifts up to place me right at her entrance.

"I need you," she whispers as she looks me in the eyes. Her big brown eyes speak to my soul. I need her too.

She slides down my shaft nice and slow. I slide my hands down her back and cup her ass. There is no rush; I intend to make love to her. This is the most tender I have ever been with Tam. We have done it slow, but this is different. My body is humming with my need for her in a soul deep way.

I move my hands once again up her back lifting her arms with me until they are above her head. I lock our fingers together and hold her gaze. Tears are spilling from both our eyes as I roll my hips up into her.

"I could never hurt you," I say as we move to our own rhythm. "I love you so much."

"I love you too," she moans, and her head falls back.

I bend my head, taking my time as I lick up the center of her chest. Her hands tighten in mine as her body quakes. I release her hands to drag my fingers down her arms, her sides and wrap them around her waist. Her body feels so good. I continue to slide in and out of her at our slow tempo. With each roll of my hip, she is rocking back into me, driving me closer to the edge. I can feel myself swelling inside her.

"Brad," she cries out, pulling my eyes from her breasts to her brown eyes that are looking back at me.

She starts to slow grind, and I swear I'm not going to last much longer like this. I move my hand over her heart and hold it there. "This is where I want to be Tamara," I say and pull her hand to my chest. "This is where you are."

I lift my hand to swipe away more tears. I pull her face to mine and fuse our lips together. I feel the moment she explodes around me, and I groan into her mouth. I am almost pulled over with her, but I grit and hold out.

"Darlin', I'm about to come. You need to get up," I grunt as I go to lift her from my shaft.

"No," she whimpers pushing back onto me. I hiss and struggle to hold back.

"I'm not wearing a condom, Baby," I say through tight lips.

"I know. I want you to come inside me," she says looking me in my eyes.

My sex clouded brain takes a few seconds to realize what she is saying to me. But when it becomes clear what Tam is offering I don't have it in me to hold back anymore. She grinds into me one last time, and I come with a force I have never known before. All I can think about is my seed planting in her belly and me getting to be there, this time, to watch her grow with my baby.

"I love you," I bellow out.

"I love you too," she whimpers into my neck.

My mind is spinning as I come down and catch my breath. She could be pregnant right now. We could be having another baby. The thought has me rock hard all over again. I swiftly switch positions, lying Tam on her back and hovering over her. I hook her legs over my shoulders and drive into her.

This is not the slow rhythm from before. The caveman within that wants her pregnant with my baby takes over. I lounge at her pussy with a mission.

"Brad," she cries out. "Oh God, what are you doing?"

"I want you pregnant I am, and I plan to make that happen tonight," I growl as I piston into her tight, wet pussy. "Fuck you feel so good."

She is so wet her tight channel is making it easy for my thick rod to slip in and out of her, but not without holding me nice and tight at the same time. I grab the hair at her nape and tip her head back as I lean in to suck on her sweat soaked neck. She is going to kill me for marking her, but I need this right now.

I need to claim what's mine in this moment. I will never willingly hurt Tam, nor am I willing to let her go. I have loved this woman for so long, even before I had her to call my own. There is no way I am fucking this up. I'll do whatever I have to, to show her what she means to me.

I growl as I thrust deep and hard. Tam arches up into me. I totally ignore the hay stabbing me from beneath the blanket. This pussy and the woman it is attached to are all that matters right now. She is mine, period. I have come too far with her to let people that don't matter, tear us apart.

"Ah, Baby, I'm so close," Tam moans.

"Give it to me Tam," I hiss in her ear. "I love this pussy. Best fucking pussy I've ever had."

"Bradley," she screams as her pussy flutters around me.

"Tam," I bellow back as I empty into her once more.

I roll to my back not breaking our connection while holding her to my chest. A few moments go by as we catch our breath. Tam tips her head up and looks at me.

"Sex is not always the answer," she says softly.

"I know baby. But this time, we both needed that," I reply and lift up to kiss her lips. "We will work through all this, but I'm not losing you, Tam. I will fight to the death for you."

She looks away from me and murmurs softly. "Be careful what you ask for."

Chapter 22

I wish it weren't so, but that engagement party has put a strain on our relationship. Only, I'm not so sure that the party is all that is to blame. Tam has been distant, and I know she is hiding something. She keeps telling me she is just nervous about the wedding and how the season will end for Ellerie and myself.

While that could be true, I'm not buying it. There is something Tam isn't telling me. I don't like it. I don't want my woman stressed while she is carrying our baby. That's right, you heard me. I'm going to be a father again. This is why at first I didn't think too much about her unusual behavior. With the morning sickness and her being so tired I had at first blamed it on the pregnancy.

However, I had a week off this weekend, and I know that something more is going on. She has been on the phone with her boss a lot. I have wondered if they are giving her a hard time at work about the upcoming wedding since she has put in for time off. Tam never takes time off, so it really shouldn't be a problem.

I'm giving her until the end of the weekend to come clean and then I am going to pull the truth from her. It has been five weeks since the engagement party. I don't like this space that seems to be between us, especially not when we should be celebrating the wedding and the baby.

We haven't told anyone though I am bursting at the seams to tell the world. I can't wait to hold my little baby in my arms. I know I can never get back the time I missed with Ellie, but I don't plan to miss a thing this time around.

I have been in the pool with Ellie all morning hoping to get my mind off things. It worked, so much that I lost track of time. I think I wore my little girl out tossing her around the pool and teaching her to perfect her backstroke. She is a natural in the water.

After getting her bathed and down for a nap, I rush to the master bedroom to get ready for the meeting I am about to be running late for. The owner of the team asked me to join him down at the yacht club today for a late lunch. I'd much rather be relaxing for the game on Monday and spending time with my family, but duty calls.

I walk into the bedroom to find Tam sitting in the middle of the bed staring down at her phone with a frustrated expression. Now that I think of it, that is the expression she has most days now when her phone is in her hands.

I know I'm going to be late now because I need to know what is going on with my woman. I climb onto the bed, and she looks up as if she is just realizing that I am in the room with her. She blinks a few times, but I don't give her time to process what is going on. I pull her into my lap and lift her face up to mine, placing a kiss to her lips.

"I think this is about enough Darlin'," I say as I pull away. "You need to tell me what is going on with you."

"I'm fine," she says looking anywhere, but in my eyes.

"Come on Tam," I sigh. "Stop lying to me. I need to know what is going on with you. It is affecting us."

She gets a sour look on her face and reaches to start twirling my hair around her finger. I start to rub circles on her back hoping to soothe her into talking to me. I give her a few minutes to open up.

"Brad, can you just trust me to handle this. It is not something I want to stress you with," she says softly.

"Anything that concerns you is a concern for me. When are you going to learn to trust me to take care of you," I ask her gently.

"I do trust you, Baby. That is not what this is about this time. I have some things I need to handle, and you need to be focused on the game. I don't want to bother you with this," she sighs and puts her head on my shoulder.

"Darlin', nothing is more important to me than you."

"Brad please, shouldn't you be off for your meeting. You are going to be late," she says lifting her head to check the time.

"Like I said, nothing is more important than you," I start, but my cell phone rings.

I take my phone out and look down at it and frown. Tam peeks at it and does the same. "Who is that?" she asks as the screen lights up with a picture of a young woman with big hair and me. I haven't a clue myself.

"I'm wondering the same thing," I murmur as I send the call to voicemail.

"How do you not know who that is? There is a picture of the two of you on your phone." Tam says, narrowing her eyes at me.

I go to answer her, but my phone rings again with the same number and photo. I want Tam to always trust me, so I answer the call and place it on speaker. Tam shifts from my lap to sit across from me cross-legged.

"Hello," I say into the phone.

"Hey honey, how are you," a woman says through the phone, with a heavy southern drawl.

Tam crosses her arms and lifts a brow at me. "I'm sorry, but who is this?" I ask.

"Aw Bradley, don't tell me you forgot about me. It's Beth, didn't my picture come up? We look so great in it," she chirps.

Tam gives me the stink eye, and I press my lips and roll my eyes at her, holding up my phone and point to the picture. I then let my mouth fall open as if to say, *'really, this looks good.'* Tam covers her mouth to stifle a laugh that bubbles up.

Beth continues, oblivious to the fact that I am not paying her any attention. "I meant to call you sooner, but I've been out of the country. I just returned last night, and I was so thrilled to hear you would be meeting on Daddy's yacht this afternoon," the woman coos.

It clicks in that moment. Beth, from the meet and greet when I found Tam and Ellie. I haven't thought about her since. I barely paid her attention that day. No wonder I didn't remember her.

"Listen, I'm already running late for that meeting. I need to go," I say as politely as I can. I have no intention of ever answering another of her calls.

"Oh, that's fine, I'll just see you when you get here," she purrs.

This gives me pause. I was told that this was just for men. I scowl and say into the phone. "Excuse me?"

"Oh, the wives decided to join you all at the last minute. Daddy thought it would be fun if I came along so you wouldn't be the odd one out," she says enthusiastically.

"Well, if they decided to invite the wives then someone should have informed me so that I could bring my fiancée," I bite out.

"Oh, you mean the lawyer," she says snidely.

The pissed look on Tam's face only pisses me off more. My blood is boiling right now. "I don't know if I sent you some type of wrong message, but I am engaged to the only woman I am interested in. You and your daddy have a good time on that boat. Something has come up. I won't be making it today," I growl before I hang up.

"Babe, you were invited by the owner to that lunch, you can't not go," Tam says with true concern in her voice.

"The hell I can't. Everyone is aware I'm engaged. Why the hell would they not tell me things have changed, let alone invite some woman along for me," I fume. "Tam if I have learned nothing else playing this sport, I have learned that the head office likes to play their own games. I go along, for the most part, but not when it comes to my family. This bull won't fly with me."

"Brad, you can't just –."

"Yes. I can," I cut her off. "Now come here. I want to rub your tummy and talk to our baby."

Chapter 23

I feel like a bull caged in a room with the walls painted red as I storm my way into the locker room. I'm so pissed off I can't even see straight. I tear into the locker room and toss my helmet at the wall. I have seen and heard a lot in this league, but this takes the cake.

I am usually the mellow guy in the locker room, so all of the guys take pause at my outburst and watch with open mouths. I turn and lock eyes with Ellerie, and he instantly reads me. I give him a curt nod and he nods back.

"Ten minutes," he says and I nod again.

I need out of this building, and I doubt it will take me ten minutes to get my shit and leave. I storm towards the shower stripping from my uniform as I go. I am showered and dressed faster than I have ever been before.

Fuming, I leave the locker room heading right for the parking lot. People are calling my name and asking questions, but I ignore them all. The only person I acknowledge is Ellerie, who is sitting in his Jaguar behind my truck, waiting for me.

"Your place," I call over my shoulder as I move past his car and jump into my own truck.

Ellerie and I have become close over the last few months, on and off the field. If I can trust anyone with what I have to say, I know it is him. I just don't want to take this to my house. Tam said she would be working from home this week, and I don't want to stress her over this.

When we pull into Ellerie's driveway, I am still wound tight and raging to release this pent up tension. I just need to say this shit out loud to make sure I haven't imagined it all. I know I did not just sit through that meeting in my coach's office. I didn't hear any of the words that were said to me. I must have gotten hit during practice or something.

"Okay, what the hell is going on," Ellerie asks as he retrieves two waters from the refrigerator and hands me one.

"They want me to postpone the wedding," I growl.

"Wait, what?" Ellerie says with a sour look on his face. He looks so much like Tam at the moment.

"Apparently that is what the head office wanted to talk to me about on that little boat trip I didn't make it to. They were going to suggest," I say using air quotes. "That I do things a little more quietly and maybe even start to be seen in public with someone else a few times. Now they just want me to postpone the wedding. 'It will be best for the rest of the season,' as they had coach put it."

"You have got to be fucking kidding. First, they fuck with Tam's clients now this," Ellerie growls causing me to almost choke on my water.

"What? What the hell did you just say," I hiss.

"Shit," Ellerie draws a hand down his face. "Listen, she didn't want to distract you from the game. She has been working to get things in order, but it has been taking its toll. The whole shit is pissing me off. The way they have been treating her at games, her losing clients that have been loyal for years.

"Tam is strong, but this is just some bullshit. I only found out by accident. They stepped to a friend of ours that wasn't willing to bend and he came to me about the situation. She is my baby sister, and I have been wanting to hurt someone over this, but she made me promise to let her handle it."

"Wait, how long has this been going on? I can't believe this; she is pregnant. She doesn't need this type of stress," I fume.

"I knew it," Ellerie says with a slight smile.

"Yeah, well, I wish I knew what was going on with Tam. I have been asking her for weeks what is going on with her. This is total bullshit."

"I hear you Brad, but understand this, she is not doing it to hurt you or because she doesn't trust you. To Tam, she sees two men, she loves on the verge of greatness, and she doesn't want to get in the way of that. I told her that she is more important to both of us than a ring, but she is determined to figure this out," he says in explanation.

"That's not going to cut it for me. I was away from my family for five years, Eli. Tam has to start opening up to me. Last time she shut me out it cost me five years with her and four with my daughter," I demand.

"I didn't say I agree with her. Listen, I have never told anyone this but there was a time when playing the game was the most important thing to me. I thought I had time for the rest.

"Boy was I wrong. I don't have to tell you what it is like to see another man with his arms around your woman. I saw your face when Mike showed up at that party. Well, I have watched more than one man hold the woman I gave up because I have been chasing my career," Ellerie snorts. "Not even a career but a ring that is never promised to any of us. Watching you and Tam just showed me what I have given up.

"It may or may not be too late for me, but I am here to make sure you and Tam don't lose sight of that. So whatever you want to do from here I am with you. At this point, a win would be bittersweet anyhow. I don't want my ring to come at the cost of my sister's happiness."

"I'm glad to hear that because your sister is about to learn just how important she is to me," I grumble.

~B~

"Tamara, I had my reasons for wanting to meet the boy. I needed to know he had integrity. I believe we should let him know what is going on here," my boss Cyrus says.

302

"I appreciate your concern Cyrus, but Brad has a team and championship to think about," I sigh.

I have been on the phone for over an hour with my boss now. My client roster is, at least, half of what it used to be. Luckily, Cyrus had the foresight to put a clause in a lot of the contracts. So while a couple of clients have left the firm altogether, others were just reassigned, as the clause wouldn't allow them to leave just yet. This includes both some of my bigger clients and some of my smaller accounts.

I have worked too hard to be going through this. I have wanted nothing more than to be a lawyer like my father since I was a little girl. Then when Ellerie got into sports, sports became my other passion. It just made sense to combine the two, but now I just think my heart isn't in it. With each passing day, I wonder if this is what I want or have I become what I thought everyone would expect of me, what would help me fit in with the guys.

I still love being a lawyer, but I don't think I would miss the over inflated egos of some of my clients. I have even toyed with the idea of being an agent, although I don't think that would fix my current problem.

Cyrus sighs heavily into the phone. "Well, I have said this a million times. I am here to help. I have set up a few meetings to get to the bottom of this. They're not the only ones that can throw some weight around."

"Cyrus," I say curiously into the phone.

"Yes Tam," he says in a soft fatherly voice.

"Why? Why do you want to help me so much? I get that you and daddy are close, old friends, but I get the sense it is bigger than that," I inquire.

There is a pause on the other end for a moment. "You know when we enter interracial relationships we do it for love. Not often do we think of what our children will look like or what their lives will be like. My first wife," his voice becomes thick with emotion."

"God, I loved her, and she was the most beautiful woman in the world to me. When I looked at her, I didn't see color or race. What I saw was a beautiful chocolate goddess that I was madly in love with. She was intelligent, fierce, loving and the warmest person you could know.

"I lost her to cancer, but not before we had three beautiful children, Tommy, Carey, and Stephanie my youngest girl.

Things became strained when we lost their mother. Stephanie, she can be sensitive. She is also the most ethnic looking of my three.

"I didn't always handle her right. When she went off to college, she fell head over heels for a young man on the basketball team. He was a nice enough young man, but after going pro, the pressure got to him. I saw it happening, and I tried to warn Stephanie. She just thought I didn't want them together. As if I, her white father had a problem with her dating a white man.

"Long story short, he broke my baby's heart. The team got in his ear, and he took the easy route. I now have a grandson that lives in Australia and a daughter that puts little effort in allowing me to see him. It also put a strain on my relationships with my other two children. Not that I don't try.

"The things they did to the two of them as a young couple. Stephanie wouldn't let me help her. With my support, the young man may have made different choices. Bradley is a different man, and you deserve to be happy Tam. Your parents raised a fine young woman.

"I have seen many things in my years, and your father has seen me through a whole lot. So I am going to see you through this," he finishes.

"Wow, Cyrus. I didn't even know you had children," I murmur in shock.

He chuckles. "You'd have to have been around the firm a pretty long time to know. Talking of my wife and children has long since become taboo. It is my hope that someday you will get to meet Stephanie and that fine young grandson of mine."

"I hope so too."

"Now back to you, take as long as you need to sort yourself out. I will handle things on this end. You just let me know if you need anything. You have options," Cyrus says.

"You know some days I just want to go home," I chuckle.

"That can be an option, Tamara. I've told you in the past I need fresh blood in New York. I would love to have a new partner there," he offers.

"Home is where the heart is, and right now my heart is in Texas," I sigh into the phone.

He chuckles again. "Be well, Dear."

I hang up the phone still not knowing what my next step is but grateful to have Cyrus in my corner. I haven't cried once throughout this mess, but suddenly the dams give way. This isn't about the money. It is about being able to do what I am good at, but most of all it is about holding on to the man that has become my rock.

~B~

Once Ellerie and I had a long talk we made some life changing decisions and started to put in calls to set things in motion. I intend to fight for Tam and her happiness. When I pull this off it is going to mean big changes for the family overall. I have no doubt I will pull this off, though.

When I get home the house is quiet, a little too quiet. If I remember correctly, Stacey was supposed to spend some time with Ellie since she is back in town. When I get to the base of the stairs, I hear loud sobbing cutting through the silence.

I start out in full run. When I make it into the room Tam is curled up in a small ball, sobbing her eyes out. My heart breaks and I know I have made the right decisions. For now, I crawl into bed and let her sob into my chest until she is ready to talk.

Chapter 24

"When were you going to tell me about losing your clients?" I say into Tam's hair as I feel her relax.

Tam huffs before turning her face up to look at me. "How did you find out?"

"Eli may have let it slip out," I shrug.

"Ugh. I should have known," she shakes her head, placing her head back on my chest she pushes her hand up under my t-shirt and starts to rub my chest. I rub her back with one hand, pushing the other into her hair to massage her scalp. "Telling you wouldn't have made any difference. It would have just distracted you. You and Ellerie have this season's win at the tips of your fingers. I have been thinking of making some changes with the baby coming anyway."

"Don't do that Tam. Don't make it seem like this is not a big deal to you. You love your job, hell you are great at it. And for the millionth time, you and our children are the most important thing in the world to me. When I wake up in the morning, you and Ellie are the first thing on my mind. Are you safe and are you happy, that is my job to know and make sure of? You have no idea how it guts me to come home and find my woman in tears.

"When I imagine what I can live without, you are not among that list. This thing that *we*," I lift her chin and point between the two of us. "Are going through, it affects our entire family, so we are going to work this out like a family. And in this family Tam, Daddy takes care of things."

I watch as heat fills her eyes at my words. I let them sink in fully as she swallows hard. I think I am finally getting through once and for all, but I know action speak louder than words. So I will prove what I mean to Tam sooner than she knows.

I continue. "You and I are getting married in just a few weeks. We are going to start our new life together and no one, and I mean no one is going to get in the middle of that. You feel me, Tam?"

"Yeah Big Country, I feel you," she says with a sultry smile.

Her hand that has been rubbing my chest makes its way confidently down to my belt, and she starts to unfasten it. I reach for her hand and still it. "Sex doesn't fix everything," I throw her own words back at her, lifting a brow at her with a teasing smirk.

"No, but good head does," she teases back and wiggles her eyebrows at me.

I release her hand without question. The things this woman can do with her mouth are amazing. Tam laughs and shakes her head at me, but she does manage to get me unfastened and out of my jeans and boxers quickly.

I don't realize I am holding my breath in anticipation until her first slow, long lick up my shaft. I heave a heavy breath and bite out a curse as she covers me with her warm mouth, sending a shudder through my body. This woman was made just for me.

~B~

I need this right now. I can be stubborn at times, but in all honesty, I love the way Brad takes charge. I can feel my whole body relax because deep inside I know he is going to make sure that everything is alright. Cyrus and Ellerie were right. I should have told Brad everything from the start.

I am not usually into men that call themselves or women that call their man Daddy, but it was so hot coming off Brad's lips that I was instantly turned on. I need to taste him, no, I need to please him. Watching Brad come apart under the ministration of my mouth is priceless.

I watch him through my lashes as I bob up and down on his length. I know his tip is extra sensitive, so I swirl my tongue around it not once but twice before sucking him in whole again. I repeat the motion, ripping a loud curse from his lips as he unfists the sheets and fists a hand full of my hair.

"Ahhh, Baby," he groans out loud.

Brad is way too thick and long for my mouth to cover him all at once, so I wrap my hands around his girth to help as I swallow him as far as I can go. He hisses out a breath as his hips buck up off the bed. I am amazed at how I can get this big man to become helpless to my oral seduction every time.

I am reminded of the first time I ever gave him head. The rush was mind blowing. The memory urges me on to make him come that hard all over again. My mouth starts to water from the thought, and I let it drip down his massive dick.

When he starts to jerk and fold into himself, I know I have him right where I want him. I let him pop free from my mouth and give his balls some much needed loving with my tongue. Brad's nostrils flare, and he groans my name in a guttural growl.

"Shit, I'm coming baby," Brad rasps, thrusting up into my mouth and holding me there as he pumps stream after stream down my throat. I swirl my tongue around him to make sure I collect all of my prize. I love the taste of my man.

Yeah, sex won't fix everything, but it sure as hell gives me a much-needed release from the stress, from what I can see the same goes for Brad. I think I know what I plan to do, starting with letting go of the worry, and focusing on the fact that I am about to get married to a man I truly love.

Chapter 25

"I want to thank you all for meeting me. This means a lot to me," I say to the men gathered around the table.

My plan is officially beginning into fall into place, and this meeting is critical to my plans. I learned a lot about Tamara's friends and her connections at Brielle's birthday party. In this room right now are the pieces I need to make some major changes in our lives.

Our wedding is in two days right before the big game. The front office isn't too happy with me, especially since I had my publicist release a statement about the upcoming wedding just to piss them off. The story of the big game has become more about whether my head will be in the game or still on my honeymoon.

They have even gone as far as making idol threats since my contract is only for one year. Originally I had agreed to the one-year contract because I knew I could get more the following year when the team freed up some money. They maxed out what they could to get me for the first year with promises of more.

I now see this all as my own bargaining chip. So their threats mean shit to me right now, especially now that I have gotten the team to the super bowl. The funny part is they know it.

"Ellerie and I have talked this over, and we feel this is something the both of us need to pursue," I continue. "Cyrus, I appreciate you making time for this. You mean a lot to Tam as her mentor and I know I can't pull this off without you."

"It's not a problem, Son. I told Tam from the beginning I would be in her corner no matter what she decided. I wanted to involve you from the beginning as well," Tam's boss Cyrus says.

I give the older man the nod and turn to the others. "Uri, Nico, and Sam thank you so much as well. I know everyone has come out for the wedding but Sam you made time for this. I appreciate that," I say to the other three men that have come to join Ellerie and myself.

"This is not a problem. Your fiancée has taken to my wife and vice versa. Tam is also important to Reese, so I know my brother is here for the same reason. Tam and Brielle's safety are important to us both. Now what is it you need," Uri responds.

I start by filling them all in on what has been going on with both Tam and I concerning my team. I can see the dark shadows that cross Uri's expression, and I wonder if I really should be calling on him. Something about the man reads deadly. Nico doesn't look any more pleased by the time I finish an account of all the events that have happened.

"So I know I need to change some things because I will not be giving Tamara up. I've waited my whole life for her and then an extra five years. When Ellerie and I thought of our options we thought of you Cyrus because Tam has worked so hard for your firm and she looks up to you," I say looking the older man in the eyes. "We then thought of you Nico and Uri from our talks at the princess party."

"Nico, I know you are looking for something new to do since retiring. As I found out more about you, Uri, I heard you and Sam Mairettie have a venture capital firm. We could probably afford to branch out into this ourselves but from what I learned, I think I can learn a lot about business from you two," I finish.

"We also have a bit of unfinished business before we can invest all of our time," Ellerie adds.

"Done," Uri states.

Sam nods. "Give me the details and we will have my brothers work out the contracts. My family is big on protecting our women, and I admire what you are willing to sacrifice," he replies.

"I think I see where you are going. I like this idea already. I'm in," Nico says with the first smile I have seen on the man's face since the day I first met him.

I feel a weight lift off my shoulders that I hadn't known was there. I am genuinely excited about this possibility now. This is going to be big, and I don't know how Tam will feel, but I know I am doing what is best for us right now.

Chapter 26

My stomach is in knots, and it has nothing to do with this pregnancy. It is the day of the big game, and my new husband will be out on that field today giving his all for a championship. He and Ellerie deserve it.

I could tell Brad was reluctant to leave last night to fly out for the game. We both agreed that I would stay home. Our house is still filled with guests from the wedding. Because of the timing we made a weekend of it. However, family and friends have been rolling in and out of the house for about a week now.

I have to admit I am happy to have everyone here around me. Something just feels off. I don't know if it is the way

Brad left, or the feeling of not having my husband here with me so soon after our wedding, or just game day jitters. I know all too well that Brad puts his life in danger every time he steps out on that field. So does my brother for that matter.

As quarterback and receiver, they might as well have targets strapped to their backs. I cringe just thinking about it. My stomach rolls and this time, it is from the baby. Boy, I don't remember being this sick with Bri. Ann and Gloria have teased that it is because I am carrying twins.

I gave them both a death glare for uttering such words. The thought has nervously crossed my mind a few times now that I know Brad's family history. Everyone was excited to find out I am expecting. We announced it at the rehearsal dinner.

Trevor cornered me after a few drinks at the wedding to tell me how sorry he was for his soon to be ex-wife. Oh yeah, after the engagement party Trevor filed for a divorce. Donna wouldn't leave without kicking and screaming, so Trevor and the kids have been staying at the family ranch.

He thought it best for the kids not to drag them in the middle of the drama as much as he could help it. Donna, on the other hand, could care less about the kids. She has still put them in the middle anyway she can, showing up at their schools and rehearsals, dropping by their friend's houses to cry victim. I feel so bad for Trevor, but he is handling it all like a boss.

I hate to call on Nico and his family and friends since Reese is still missing, but Val insisted Trevor contact Mairettie and Mairettie for the divorce. Obviously, Donna rubbed a few people the wrong way. I know Trevor is in good hands.

I pat my queasy stomach and smile. I hadn't realized how big my support team has grown over the years. I guess that is why what should have been a small intimate wedding still turned out to be over a hundred people. Heck, my extended family, through Reese and Nico alone, could have filled an entire section.

I am grateful to have them all here right now. I think Brielle is overjoyed as well, as all her real cousins and cousins through close parental relationships storm the house with her. I shake my head to think that I am having another little monster. With all these kids here, I really think I have gone crazy.

"Here, you look like you could use this," Stacey runs a hand over my hair and hands me a pack of crackers and some ginger ale.

"You're the best," I smile as I take the crackers and tear into them, "Didn't think we'd be doing this again."

We both fall into a fit of giggles. "Yeah, I know, and certainly not with your husband of all people. I'm so happy for you Tamara."

"I'm still pinching myself," I admit as I look around at the people in our home laughing and enjoying themselves.

"So does that mean you're finally ready to thank me for making you go out that night," Stacey says with a toothy grin.

"No heifer, you left me with a stranger to chase down the D," I grumble playfully.

"Ah, oh yes, Troy. I remember that fine man. I still don't remember why I stopped taking his calls," Stacey frowns in thought. Blowing out a breath and waving the thought off she moves on. "This has to be bittersweet for you guys. I mean with the team and the drama they tried to cause you guys. This all must suck for Brad."

"Yeah, pretty much. He and Ellerie want and deserve a ring, but winning means giving the club a win. What are you going to do," I shrug.

This is a thought that has been on my mind, but I would never ask Brad not to play or not to win for his team just to spite a bunch of spiteful people. I guess we have to pick and choose our battles. I won't lie, though, a part of me wishes he and Ellerie gave the team the finger and walked away.

"Well, I'm proud of you for hanging in there. I know this has been tough. Add on the wedding and the baby, I have no idea how you pulled this all off," Stacey shakes her head.

"I didn't do it alone. All of you guys have been so helpful. I just wish Reese were here," I sigh as I think of my friend.

Stacey makes a face and starts to fidget in her seat. I narrow my eyes at her. Oh no, these heifers don't. My mouth falls open, and I snatch Stacey by the collar, pulling her closer to me. "You know where she is," I hiss in her face.

I have felt so bad for Nico. I can't believe Stacey knows where she is and hasn't said anything. I want to strangle her.

"Relax," Stacey whispers looking around as she pries my fingers from her blouse. "I don't know where she is. She won't give me a location, but I know that she is okay. She had me stream the wedding to her through my phone."

"What?" I ask in confusion.

"You know you are her girl. She feels terrible about not making the wedding, but she wanted to be there. I told Brad some lame story about my grandma not being able to make it, but wanting to stream it, and he had it set up for me," she goes on to explain.

"And why the hell has she been in contact with you and not me," I pout.

Stacey shrugs. "She knows you and Val have become close. If Uri gets wind that any of us knows a thing, he is going to help Nico drag her ass back here."

"Well, it is where she belongs," I huff. "He loves her. I can't believe she is doing this."

"It is deeper than that, and you know it. I think I can understand what she is doing. I may not agree, but I understand. I haven't said anything because I think it will all work itself out just like with you and Brad," Stacey says wistfully.

I go to interrogate Stacey further, but Brielle comes running in the room. "Mommy, Pop-pop said to tell you to come here, now! Daddy is on TV," Bri says as she tries to catch her breath.

That feeling in my gut squeezes at me again. I rush to the family room where my mom and Gloria have been setting up for the game. When I make it to the room, it seems like everyone is already piled in with their eyes glued to the TV.

I look at the screen, and Brad and Ellerie are sitting in a press conference. I know right away something isn't right. Someone turns the TV volume up, and I try to force the panic back so that I can focus on their words.

"Bradley, is it true you will not be playing today in the super bowl championship game," a reporter calls out on the screen.

"Yes, that is true. I have decided that I want to sit out the rest of the season," Brad replies.

"Ellerie, you too won't be playing," another reporter asks sounding confused.

"Nope, I will not be playing either for personal reasons," Ellerie smiles into the camera.

"But you two are an intricate part of this organization. It can be said that you two are the reason this team is in the super bowl at all," yet another voice says.

Brad leans forward into the mic. "I believe the organization will be fine without our help today," Brad says shyly.

"Bradley, Brad. I have just heard a rumor that you are considering signing a new contract with New York," a reporter blurts above the other voices.

"Rumors are rumors, you guys know that," Brad says with a devilish smile that makes me gasp. I have no idea what is going on. "However, my contract here was only for a year, so my options are open."

"Ellerie you are going to be a free agent as well aren't you? My sources say that New York may be courting you guys as a package deal."

"Even if such talk was going on in the background, I don't kiss and tell guys. I can tell you this. I just want to take this time to be as healthy as possible for next season. Retirement will be looking good soon and I just want to end my career healthy and happy," Ellerie says smoothly.

"Does this have anything to do with you getting married this past week, Bradley?"

"No, my wife is back home finding out about all this along with you guys. She is probably just as shocked," Brad chuckles. "I won't lie. I can't wait to get back home to her and my family. Tamara Monroe is my world. Recent events have put this fact to the test, and I hope that everyone has gotten the message, but I am making this decision for me. A man has to know when to be a man."

"That sounds really personal, Brad. What is really happening in the camp to cause this upset," one of the reporters pounce.

Brad shrugs and sits back in his seat. "I came home to find myself. This is me, has nothing to do with anyone else."

"I'm not buying that," one of the reporters snorts. "Ellerie, Tamara is your sister, isn't she? You are both choosing not to play. I don't think it is a coincidence."

"Believe what you want," Ellerie shrugs. "Bottom line is we are not playing. We wish our teammates well and know that they for the most part understand."

"We have a plane to catch guys. Thank you so much," Brad says and stands to leave as the reports frantically call out more questions. My husband walks off camera like a boss, my brother doing the same and both look damn good doing it.

The commentators on the sports channel come back on and start to speculate on why the guys won't be playing. They are excitedly talking about the rumors that both Brad and Ellerie will be signing to a New York team. My heart is pounding, and my head is spinning.

I haven't asked Brad about what we were going to do about all of this since the afternoon he found me in bed crying. I decided to let him handle it, and I have been focused on the wedding. I still don't know what all this means. I stumble to the nearest chair and have a seat.

"Looks like we're all going home," Stacey says with a dubious smile.

I look at her and blink. "I never knew leaving Texas was an option," I say in almost a whisper.

"Tam, when it comes to you Brad will make anything an option," Stacey chirps.

"Yeah, I get that now," I nod and absently rub my still flat belly. My brother and husband just gave up a chance at winning the super bowl for me.

~B~

"Monroe, I don't know what the fuck you think you are pulling here," the GM of the team bellows as he barrels toward Ellerie and me.

"I'm not pulling anything. I am well within my right not to play tonight. Just like you are well within your right to fine me if you like," I smile.

I could give two shits about a fine or about not playing tonight. I have a ring, and I know I can make it to the championship again, where I plan on going. Even if I don't win another one, so be it. I love my wife more than anything, and no one is going to get away with hurting her or her career without me having a say.

Ellerie, on the other hand, has made a big sacrifice here and as a brother, I know I would do the same for Trevor or Ann in a heartbeat. The GM glares at me and then looks at Ellerie. Ellerie just glares back daring him to test him. Ellerie has been known to speak up when he feels something isn't right or that the team isn't treating him fair. So I know the GM is not going to willingly go there with him right now.

"You two are unbelievable. You pick game day to pull this shit," he growls.

"You picked weeks before my wedding to demand I not marry the love of my life. You picked the first trimester of my wife's pregnancy to threaten her clients into leaving her. You picked my engagement party to help my sister in law pay for that plane ticket for my ex to crash the event," I bellow.

At his shocked expression, I snort. "Yeah, I found out everything. You, boys, have been very busy. Have a nice game."

I shove past the dick that is standing with his mouth flapping open like a fish out of water. I have a wife to get home to. We have a lot of packing to do.

Chapter 27

Brad text me that he and Ellerie were boarding a flight home. I have been going out of my mind with questions since the press conference. They had the interview playing on repeat during the entire game. Needless to say that Brad was being blamed for his team taking an epic L.

I was a little shocked at the support that Brad was receiving, though. It seems that speculations of Brad wanting to leave the team were already floating around the league. Rumors of the club having it out for Brad had gotten out there; he is receiving support from players, coaches and commentators alike, who have known him and know he is a great guy and dedicated player.

I was floored and brought to tears when a few of my loyal clients defended Brad. Without giving details, they said they understood why Brad did what he did, and they would have done the same. Ellerie wasn't off the hook, they had comments on his refusal to play, but Brad was taking the brunt of it being the team quarterback and captain.

The family watched more of the newscasts on the developments with Brad than the actual game. More than a few of us had questions about what was going on. Once the shock wore off, I helped Gloria, and my mom get everyone fed and distracted with games and movies.

I was so grateful to my dad and Vernon when they started to clear people out and guide the remaining guests that were staying at the house to their rooms. Ann was kind enough to take Ellie with her for the night, even though she would be sharing taking care of Ellie for the next two weeks while Brad and I are away on our honeymoon.

It is already late, and I have been wearing a hole in the floor with Six at my feet. I have to say I have become attached to the little puppy. My head snaps up, and I am pulled from my thoughts as I hear heavy footfalls, and Six takes off for the bedroom door.

The doors are pulled open, and Brad squats down to rub the top of Six's head. "Hey buddy, you keeping Mama safe," he coos to the dog before his bright blue eyes look up at me.

"I don't know about safe, but he has been some company while I have been wondering what has been going on," I say tilting my head at him.

Brad lifts to his full height, closing the doors behind him and strolls easily over to me. He cups the back of my head and wraps an arm around my waist pulling me in for a hot, possessive kiss. I feel my toes curl in my slippers. My arms go around his neck, and I hold on tight.

"Hello, wife," Brad murmurs against my lips as he breaks the kiss.

"Hello, husband," I laugh back at him. "Are you going to explain what happened today?"

"I sure am," he says while walking me back toward the bed and nuzzling my neck.

"Will that be before or after you ravish me?" I ask breathlessly with a small laugh on my lips.

"I would prefer after, but I don't know if you'll let me get away with that," he teases.

331

"Nope, not a chance, spill country boy," I tease back.

Brad mock sighs and places his forehead to mine. "I love you," he says as his intense stare send chills through me. I nod because I am becoming too emotional.

Brad shucks off his suit jacket and tosses it to the chair before sitting at the foot of the bed and pulling me into his lap. "I told you from the beginning I would take care of you and our family. To me, that means making sure you are not disrespected or taken advantage of. I was willing to deal with the club when they were just targeting me, but when I found out that they were messing with your career all bets were off.

"I put it all out there on the field this season. Getting that team to the championships was not easy. For them to think after all of that, they could disrespect my woman," he pauses and frowns, shaking his head. "Not gonna happen Darlin'. Not on my watch. I only signed with the team for a one-year contract as you know. I had every intention back then to sign on to a longer contract for next season.

"Once I really started to dig into things, I realized that the team had problems with our relationship for some time. So I had to make a few decisions. When I first started to feel homesick, New York was one of the first teams that tried to court me. They actually offered me more than Texas had, but I wanted to come home to be with my family.

"I made a few calls, and they are still interested. When I mentioned that my one condition was that they sign Ellerie as well since his contract is also up this season, they jumped at it. I'm still young, and I want out while I can still play the game with our son," Brad gives me a sly smile and rubs his hand over my tummy.

"Even if I signed a longer contract here, I wouldn't have committed to more than two or three more years. I wanted a family and to settle down. I have that now, so my new contract will be a two-year contract with a one-year option."

"Really Brad, I just never thought about you not playing, you love the game. I didn't think leaving Texas was an option either. Your whole family is here," I muse out loud in shock.

"I love the game, but not more than my girls. You and Ellie mean the world to me, which is why I made this choice. I love being here in Texas where my family is but moving to New York doesn't mean we have to give up our home here. We can come see the family whenever we want. I also want to see you happy. I know your career has been here in Texas, so

I called in a few favors, and I have a surprise for you," Brad says with a shy smile.

"Well, you are just full of those today," I laugh.

"I have movers coming in while we are on our honeymoon to pack this place up. Trevor and the kids are going to move in here for the time being until he gets things settled with the divorce. I've rented a place until we can find something of our own, but we can take our time with that.

"You are probably going to be pretty busy as one of the new partners at our firm in New York," he says while watching my eyes closely.

"What?" I gasp and furrow my brows.

Brad smiles. "I talked with Cyrus a bit. He told me he had been toying with the idea of a New York office. After talking with Nico at Ellie's party, I realized he might be onto something with wanting to manage other players. Not to mention, I got excited talking to Uri about a venture capital group for athletes that want to expand their portfolios.

"After having a meeting with them all we came up with a New York Office that you and Nico will run, with Uri and Cyrus's connections and backing. In a year, Ellerie and I will come on as agents," he says smiling broadly at his accomplishments.

"I don't even know what to say," I shake my head with a smile on my lips.

"Say you'll follow your country boy husband to the big city," Brad smiles.

"I will follow your big country ass to the ends of the earth, Bradley Monroe," I say with a big grin on my face.

"That's what I want to hear. Now come give your husband some of that good pussy, Tam. I'm starving for you," he says huskily.

So that is exactly what I do. It was my intention to rock Brad's world, but he flipped mine inside out. I'm sure our guests were ready to make their way home by the morning. In the moment, though, I didn't care, Brad and I had been through a lot, and we were coming out on the other side together and stronger for it.

My lesson in all of this was that I don't have to do it all alone. Brad may be younger, but he is a take charge man. Once he wants something nothing will stop him from having it. I should have known that from the first night I met him. If you would have told me then that I would have taken him home and someday would be calling that young rookie my husband, I would have laughed in your face.

Not so much because he was white, but in truth because I Tamara Monroe used to need to control everything. Now I know how to be a boss, but let my captain steer the ship every once in a while. We both make mistakes, but the best part is getting to fix them with the support of one another.

Epilogue

I feel when Brad walks up behind me. I sag into his chest as he wraps his arms around me. I have the best husband a woman can ask for. I love my life. It has been almost two years since we got married. So much has changed, but our lives could not be happier.

"They are growing up so fast," I sigh as I watch the Twins roll around with their new puppy. Brielle is laying on her back in the grass giggling while Six licks all over her face.

"Exactly why I am so happy we are having another one," Brad kisses my neck and rubs my tummy.

"Do you miss it?" I ask. Brad stayed true to his word. He played for one year in New York, brought home a ring for him and Ellerie and retired.

"The game or New York," he asks.

"Both," I shrug. The firm in New York has been a big success, but we just moved back here to Texas a few weeks ago. It's not permanent we just thought we should spend at least the summer here with the family. We will decide how much time we will split between the two in the fall.

Things in New York will be fine without me. Ellerie has really taken a large role in handling the office. He loves it. Nico's Brother, Michael, has been very instrumental as well. While I love our life in New York, this right here is something special.

I can't wait for the twins to be old enough for us to go riding as a family. Ashley and Ashton are just about the cutest little ones ever. I finally have a child that looks like me. Ashton may have his father's personality, but he has my eyes and smile, he is mama's boy all the way. Brad and I make some beautiful babies.

"Honestly, I think I'm good on the game. I'd much rather spend time with you and the kids. As for New York," he shrugs. "You can take the boy out of the country, but not the country out of the boy. Our circle there is great, but I love this, the fresh air, the open space, the fact that my family is not that far when I need alone time with my wife."

"Oh please Brad, my parents had the kids just about every weekend," I laugh and turn in his arms to look up at him.

"Yeah, but my parents have them during the week, and Ann has them on the weekends here," I throw my head back and laugh harder.

"Well, enjoy it while it lasts we'll be back in the busy city in no time. I think it's time to look for a bigger place, by the way," I say thoughtfully.

"Already taken care of Darlin'," Brad smiles at me sheepishly. "Just in case, we have another set of twins."

"Shut your mouth," I swat his arm playfully.

"I love you, Tam. I'm glad I found my way back to you," Brad says suddenly more intense than before.

"I love you too, Brad. More than you could ever know."

ACKNOWLEDGMENTS

This book was different and fun for me. I hope that you enjoyed it. I want to thank you guys that have become loyal readers and those of you that have just found my books as well. It is a pleasure to share with you all. Thanks for the LOL moments and the well wishes on Facebook as well.

Thank you to the home crew that supports me in all of this. You guys are the bomb. I can't begin to tell you how grateful I am. I have wanted to write books since I was a little girl and to be doing so and have such a great response is awesome to me. I have been through college and have two Masters Degrees, but this right here brings a smile to my face and brings me so much joy. I love to create, and I love that you enjoy what I create. So thank you so much, with all my heart.

Once again to God, be all the Glory for my talent and the courage not to bury it. I thank him for taking me out of my box and showing what I can really do. I am nothing and can do nothing without the source of my being.

It is that time, on to the next!

ABOUT THE AUTHOR

Blue Saffire is a housewife with too much time to think and not enough time to herself. By some miracle, she has found the time to write books. Blue represents the secret author inside that some of us are too scared to let out.

Blue is a loving wife, who is itching to make her way back to city life. The burbs are not enough background music to the story of her life. Life throws Blue challenges daily and since her diary is no longer enough, she has decided it is time for a new outlet. Thus, you are gaining access to the mind of Blue Saffire.

So here in lays the thoughts of Blue Saffire, the author, the wife, and the woman. Enjoy.

Would you like to meet Blue Saffire in person, along with her bestselling author friends S.K. Lessly and Tiffany Patterson?

Well, join her at Blue's March Madness in 2017

See you there!

Wait there is more to come! You can stay updated with my latest releases by subscribing to my newsletter at

www.BlueSaffire.com

If you enjoyed Ballers, I'd love to hear

your thoughts and please feel free to leave a

review for it. And when you do, please let me

know by emailing me TheBlueSaffire@gmail.com

or leave a comment on Facebook https://www.facebook.com/BlueSaffireDiaries or Twitter @TheBlueSaffire

To reach my PR team please contact

Angelle Barbazon

JKS Communications - Literary Publicity

angelle@jkscommunications.com

Other books by Blue Saffire

Placed in Best Read Order

Also available....

Legally Bound

Legally Bound 2: Against the Law

Legally Bound 3: His Law

Perfect for Me

Hush 1: Family Secrets

Ballers: His Game

Brothers Black 1: Wyatt the Heartbreaker

Legally Bound 4: Allegations of Love

Hush 2: Slow Burn

Coming Soon…

Brothers Black 2: Noah …October 2016

Legally Bound 5.2: Camille

Brothers Black 3